It's Our Time
Diane Krauss

It's Our Time

Diane Krauss

It's Our Time

Diane Krauss

Zimbell House Publishing
Union Lake, Michigan

This book is a work of fiction. Any references to historical events, real people, or real locales are used fictitiously. All characters appearing in this work are the product of the author's imagination, and any resemblance to actual persons, living or dead is entirely coincidental.

All rights reserved, including the right of reproduction in whole or in part in any form. No part of this publication may be reproduced, distributed, or transmitted in any form or by any means, including photocopying, recording, or other electronic or mechanical methods, without the written permission of the publisher.

For permission requests, write to the publisher
"Attention: Permissions Coordinator"
Zimbell House Publishing
PO Box 1172
Union Lake, Michigan 48387
mail to: info@zimbellhousepublishing.com

© 2019 Diane Krauss

Published in the United States by Zimbell House Publishing
http://www.ZimbellHousePublishing.com
All Rights Reserved

Hardcover ISBN: 978-1-64390-043-8
Trade Paper ISBN: 978-1-64390-044-5
.mobi ISBN: 978-1-64390-045-2
ePub ISBN: 978-1-64390-046-9
Library of Congress Control Number: 2019902960

First Edition: July 2019
10 9 8 7 6 5 4 3 2 1

Zimbell House Publishing
Union Lake

Dedication

A special thank you to my mother for being my biggest fan. This book is dedicated to my husband and our son, for whom my heart beats.

"... That whenever any Form of Government becomes destructive of these ends, it is the Right of the People to alter or to abolish it, and to institute new Government, laying its foundation on such principles and organizing its powers in such form, as to them shall seem most likely to effect their Safety and Happiness. ..."-The Declaration of Independence

Chapter One

Brooklyn 2046

Don't get your hopes up.
 It is the future, but I can bet it isn't how you imagined it would be.
 There aren't any flying cars or talking robots. Cyborgs and teleportation are still science fiction. The truth is most of us are lucky if we eat a hot meal every day. Some homes have four walls and a roof, some don't. The water is tainted, so is the food. Violent crime is up at a record high, and hospitals are overcrowded. There are no jobs because there is no money. Not for us anyway.
 These truths are part of the reason why I am running for my life right now. But the people chasing me aren't your everyday criminals. This isn't a mugging, which in Brooklyn, let's be honest, is quite common to see.
 Damn.
 I could kick myself for being so naive.
 Deep down I knew there couldn't be peace between us. When a group has power for as long as they have, it's not something that they will easily part with. Now I am a threat to the world they created—a world that lives and breathes to serve them. Their mansions, private jets, yachts, and the unlimited funds in their bank accounts are all in jeopardy because of me—or us, really. Yet I still thought coming here to try my hand at diplomacy was a good idea.

You would think the realities of the world would have hardened me by age twenty, but despite all the horrors I had witnessed I still believed there could be a happy ending for everyone. Perhaps that was my mother in me. My father, on the other hand, would have hit me upside the head for coming here.

No, these men chasing me aren't strangers. They're the same men who were supposed to be protecting me. They're the United States Secret Service. They're dressed in all black, but not like Will Smith in that oldies film. These men wear long black leather coats even in the summer. Their collars extend high on their necks and are accented with fur at the brim. Their black cotton shirts, black denim pants, and black combat boots complete the uniform.

As for me, I typically wear one of my father's old work T-shirts imprinted with the logo "Logan & Co." paired with weathered cargo pants. Today for the meeting I wore a skirt and heels for the first time in my entire life. I couldn't regret that more right now. The alternative to running in heels is running barefoot, and in a world that hasn't had garbage pickup in years, I wouldn't recommend it.

The alleyway is wide, and each turn I take brings me to a new alley, all of which are cluttered by the broken glass and debris that litter the rest of the world. The large mounds of garbage are the only things protecting me. I hear them fire two shots, but my guess is they can't get a lock on me. I'm trying to stay low as I run and keep covered behind the heaping trash, but I don't see an end to this. I can't outrun them. When I looked back last, there were five of them on my tail. I turn back again, but I only see three this time. I round another corner and continue to run but stop dead in my tracks.

A dead end.

No!

The brick wall extends three stories high on all sides of me. There is a ladder on the wall in front of me. It looks like an old fire escape, but I won't be able to climb it before they round the corner. There's a door to the left.
I try to open it.
It's locked!
I can feel my heart beating in my ears. I turn around, and the three men in uniform are lined up blocking my only way out. *They're going to kill me.*
No, it's worse.
They still haven't taken their shot.
Their orders must have been to take me in alive. They're going to make me their Puppet. Then what will happen to everyone else?
Dad.
Theo.
Lou.
I can't think about them now. I kick off my shoes.
Climb!

Chapter Two

Brooklyn 2044

I know how it sounds, but Brooklyn isn't all that bad. Before it was trendy, before the reformers and Divisions, it was just Brooklyn. My home. We were in Brownsville Brooklyn, which is far from the affluent neighborhoods of Dumbo and Brooklyn Heights. We had been the murder capital of NYC since my dad was born in 1990. Due to Brownsville's lack of appeal, we managed to keep the city to ourselves for a long time, but like everything, eventually, things changed.

My family had lived in Brooklyn since my great-great grandfather moved there in 1946 after the war. In 2026, the year I was born, my father started his own construction company, Logan & Co. The economy was on the rise and Brooklyn was thriving—the entire nation was. My brother was born when I was two-years-old. That was the last year we had a democratic election.

2028 was the year the reformers took office, or as we called them, the Elites. The Elites believed in a government-run society—essentially, a welfare state. Their leader, a woman named Torrent, campaigned on the promise of social equality, universal healthcare, and fortified government housing and food programs. They've been in office ever since, and sixteen years later here we are.

Brownsville. Division 12. Home.

The hipsters don't bother me much. Normally they seem to be in their own world anyway. They support the Elites. Under the Elites' administration, almost every aspect of the Constitution was modified. Drugs and prostitution were legalized, and gun ownership was forbidden. Hospitals and supermarkets began to operate under the government, and eventually, private stores were banned altogether. It didn't happen overnight, but it happened quickly. By the time I turned eight, society was divided into two groups, which eventually became known as the Elites and the Hoodlums. At first, there were uprisings by the Hoodlums, but those who held different beliefs from the government were quickly arrested and made examples of by long prison sentences. Then, prisons were closed down completely because living in the cities outside of the Elites' walls was punishment enough.

From my window, I could see the subway station. The walk there was under ten minutes from my house, which was great for me because I was always running late.

"Bye Nana," I said, leaning over her bed and giving my grandmother a kiss on the cheek. "I made coffee for you, and there is toast in the toaster."

Nana opened one eye. "Why don't you stay home and take care of your poor grandmother instead?" She glanced up at me from under her sheets trying to look innocent.

"I would love nothing more than to stay home with you my *sweet* Nana, but you aren't sick." I emphasized the word "sweet" because she and I both knew it wasn't the adjective that best described her.

"Yeah, yeah this whole world is sick," Nana mocked, waving her hand. "Be careful," she warned as she kicked her covers off and sat up. For eighty-years-old, she was in great shape.

"I will, Nan. Love you," I replied.

She fiddled her feet around at her bedside to find her slippers as I walked out of the room. This conversation played out almost every day. Nana had only left the apartment a handful of times during the six years she had lived with us. She was a small and stout woman, no taller than five feet, but she packed a mighty punch. She raised my mother and aunt by herself in a small town in upstate New York. My parents insisted she move in with us after my aunt passed away six years ago. Nan didn't want to come to the city, but she didn't really have a choice.

I grabbed my hat and stopped off in the kitchen to say bye to Lou before I left. She should have been done eating by now, but Lou worked at her own pace. I signed, "Bye Lou Lou."

She was still eating the breakfast that I had put out for her twenty minutes ago. It was half a cup of oatmeal with a glass of skim milk.

"Finish eating ... you can't miss the bus again, and you still have to brush your teeth," I signed.

Lou nodded her head and smiled, scooping a spoonful of oatmeal into her mouth.

I headed down the stairs of my building. As I walked by each apartment, I could hear vids playing the morning news or something or another on the One Network. Vids were modern versions of the old-fashioned television, and the One Network was the one and only broadcasting network we had. Don't get me wrong, there were plenty of channels to watch including a variety of news, sitcoms, and talk shows, but they were all censored and monitored by the Network's owners, the U.S. government. The key feature of each vid was its ability to automatically turn on to broadcast live announcements from the president.

Not everyone had a vid in their home. Ours was old and only worked when it wanted to. For the people who didn't have one, there were ividcams on every fourth corner throughout each Division in every state across the U.S. Mostly they were used to broadcast the president's speeches or emergency announcements. The ividcam was essentially a three-dimensional hologram projection with both visual and audio features. The closest one to us was one block north of our building. The hologram could be projected as high as forty feet so nobody would have a problem viewing it; the government made sure of that.

President Torrent and her establishment operated out of a high-rise tower located on the Lower East Side of what used to be Manhattan. It was called Torrent Tower. It wasn't in an Elite Village nor did a wall protect it. It was the largest building left in the city, and it was different than the other towers that remained—it was white.

I knew from my dad that the United States president used to work out of Washington D.C. in a place called the White House, but that city had long been obsolete to the Elites. Washington D.C. was now a war-torn ghetto known as Division X. I had never been there, nor did I have any desire to go. I just stayed right here in Brooklyn where I had always been.

I knew everyone in our building. We lived on the second floor of a three-story walk up. There were sixteen apartments in total, but ten of them were vacant. The housing was completely subsidized—monthly dues were determined by income, age, and health. My family paid two hundred dollars per healthy person of working age—Theo, my mother, and me—and one hundred dollars for everyone else, meaning Nan, Dad, and Lou. This covered rent, cable, and tickets to the Rations Center for food and clothing. Nine hundred dollars might not seem like a lot, but with only one income coming in for the household, we just barely covered the monthly fee.

In our building, there were the Carters on the first floor, and Emily and Russ on the third along with the Adersons, Paul and Mabel. Rose Keller was on the ground floor; she had just had a baby. Mr. Maxwell and his grandson, Kai, were on the second floor with us.

Kai is my age, and he is my best friend. He moved in to take care of his grandfather six years ago after his parents passed away. Looking at him you would think he was an Elite. His dark blonde hair fell just below his ears, and his almond-shaped eyes were the lightest shade of hazel. His body was slender but strong. No matter what he wore, he looked put together, which was a gift I didn't possess.

I rounded the corner on the ground floor and saw Rose with her baby carriage struggling to open the front door. "I got it!" I exclaimed as I started a light jog toward the door, which was only about ten feet away. I opened it wide.

Rose was only a few years older than me. She was a petite woman with blonde hair and plain features. Her brown eyes looked weary for her age.

I lifted the front end of the baby carriage with one arm and held the door open with the other, as Rose wriggled the carriage into the building. "Oh El, thank you! I owe you my life!" she cried, as she released her hands from the carriage and pulled me in for a hug while still in the doorway. I laughed while I hugged her back using my foot to hold the door.

"Were you standing out there for that long?" I asked, chuckling.

"No! Thanks again for the baby formula you gave us, by the way!" she smiled, still holding my arms in her hands. "Emma has been sleeping and eating finally. It's like a miracle!" Rose shook her head and shrugged her shoulders up high to her ears. With a deep sigh, she relaxed her shoulders and her grip. "Thank you," she repeated.

I peeked into the carriage to see Emma who was smiling up at me. "Attagirl Emma," I said. I reached down and rubbed her cheek as she let out a giggle, then I straightened and looked back up at Rose. "Oh, hey …

why don't you come over for some tea later?" I asked, remembering that Mom had been asking about her. "I know Mom and Nana would love to see you two."

"That sounds lovely El, thank you," she replied warmly. Rose had been living alone since her husband passed away during her first trimester. I imagined how lonely she must have been.

"Okay, great! We'll see you later, then," I said, smiling and leaning down to the baby carriage one more time. "And you too!" I added, while lightly poking Emma's tiny button nose. I waved as Rose walked into the building toward her apartment then I turned and continued on my way.

Work had been busy, which wasn't anything new. Almost all the inner cities were war zones even though One Network tried to portray it otherwise. The crime rate had been on a steady incline since 2024, which meant I would never be out of work. Sometimes I felt like I just stitched people up to send them back out into the battlefield.

If it wasn't the gangs killing each other, then it was the drugs. Most drugs were legal and available without a prescription at the Rations Center. That's where my parents were now. They weren't getting drugs though; they were getting food. It was the second Monday of the month, which meant it was Rations Day for J-L. They'd been out since early this morning trying to beat the lines. Brooklyn had twelve Divisions, also known as the Slums, each of which had its own Rations Center. We were the twelfth. Each of those divided their ration days by last name. Still, each line could be 15,000 people deep, and with only four or five lines you can do the math. I could picture my dad waiting patiently in line.

Before my dad started his construction company, he was in the Army. He joined in 2008 when he was eighteen to fight the War on Terrorism in the Middle East. He worked his way up the ranks for seven years until he was wounded in a roadside bomb. His truck flipped and rolled over into an embankment puncturing his lung, so the military sent him home.

The Rations Center hired old military personnel for security, so my dad knew a few of the men there. Dad applied for employment at the center, but he was declined for failing the aptitude test. The test began specifically for Torrent's Secret Service decal. She expected complete loyalty and obedience from the people who surrounded her. The men who passed the test began working as her Secret Service. She called them her Mules. She had one Mule who she favored most, called the Elk. These men along with Bruna, her assistant, were the closest people to Torrent. All government security positions require the aptitude test now. By the look of most of the security officers and cops around here, I was convinced they only hired morons.

Dad never received special treatment down at the Rations Center, and he didn't ask for it either. The only time we got something extra was on Dad's birthday, when his old friend Caleb, a security officer at our Center, gave our family cake rations even when we weren't eligible. The man could have gotten fired for something so simple.

Dad and Caleb go way back. Apparently, Dad pulled a wounded Caleb out of enemy fire when they unknowingly walked into a trap while searching a building in Afghanistan. I'd say that earned Dad a cake once a year. I get it though. These men are just doing their jobs, and most of them are just thankful to have one.

It was a warm day in the city. At only eight in the morning, the sun was shining in a lightly clouded blue sky. You'd think that such weather would be welcome, but the smell of hot steel and garbage was only more potent in the sun. The spring air hit my skin like a warm embrace, and I breathed it in. Okay, so maybe it's not the freshest air, in fact, the smell turned my stomach, and I wrinkled my nose and exhaled sharply, but it's what we've got. I had always been pretty good at making the best of a situation.

I turned and looked back at my building. It wasn't much to look at. The bricks were worn from the elements, moss and weeds had taken over much of its north side. My parents' room and Theo's room faced the north, but the rest of the apartment looked out to the east, which was the direction I was walking. I glanced back at the building and caught a glimpse of Nana watching me out of the kitchen window. I saw Mr. Carter rounding the corner onto our street.

"Good Morning, El!" he exclaimed, hiking his cane in the air in a mini-salute. His warm smile displayed all four of the teeth that were left in his mouth.

"Morning Mr. Carter," I smiled.

"When are you coming up to help me in the garden? The cherry tomatoes came in!" Mr. Carter said with a grin.

He and his wife had an impressive greenhouse on the roof. They had always loved to garden. When I was little, he used to take me up there, and I would help water and weed the plants. He would let me take one vegetable of my choice home with me each week in exchange for my help. I always chose the tomatoes—they were my favorite.

I would spend countless hours up there in the spring and summer, whether it was helping Mr. Carter or simply reading and writing. The rest of the world seemed to disappear when I was up there. I would stick my face in the tomato vines and breathe them in. That smell could instantly take me back to my childhood.

"I'll come up this week, okay?" I said, reaching out to touch his forearm.

Mr. Carter is old but not elderly by any means. His wit is sharp, and he could run circles around some of these young kids today. "That's not an answer," he said. "You'll come up tomorrow," he added with a raise of his brow and a wink.

"I'll come up tomorrow," I said with a playful roll of my eyes and a nod.

"See you tomorrow, Ms. Logan! And be careful out there," he warned, patting my hand then pausing a beat. It seemed like he had something else to say, but he released my hand and continued to walk away.

"I will see you later!" I called to him and then turned to continue to walk my direction.

The world was a dangerous place. I knew from the stories Nana told me that there were always dangerous places, but it was different now. It was dangerous *everywhere*. When we were kids, my brother and I used to ride our bikes around the neighborhood, and before we went home, we would always stop at the local deli for a fifteen-cent cookie. By the summer that I turned twelve, the price of a cookie was more than my parents could afford to spare. Eventually, private stores would go out of business completely giving way solely to the government-run Rations Centers. However, the two coexisted for a while.

Theo and I had started going to the ration line for our cookies. A family of five got a box of twenty cookies bi-monthly. They might as well have been made of dirt because that's what they tasted like.

One day, we decided to feed them to the ducks down at the park across the street. There were a group of kids not too much older than us who always hung around down there. I kept my distance, but no matter what I said or how many times I said it my brother always seemed intrigued by them. There was a boy, Salazar, who seemed to be the leader. He was fourteen-years-old, and although there were older kids, Salazar seemed to be the one calling the shots. Soon, Theo started hanging around them. They smoked cigarettes and listened to loud music. They were part of a gang called BK12.

One day my brother came home with a box of deli cookies. I didn't ask how he got them. When our parents found out that he stole them they were furious. I felt responsible for Theo since he was my little brother after all, so I took the blame. I was grounded for a month—no cookies, no park, no anything. Theo stopped taking bike rides with me that year. No one in my family really saw much of him after that summer.

In our apartment, there was my mom and dad, Nana, Theo, Lou, and me. Lou was short for Louise, but I don't think I called her that in all her seven years. It was just like everyone called me El, short for Elisha. We had a three-bedroom one-bathroom apartment. It may sound crowded for six people but to be honest, everywhere was either crowded, demolished, or both.

The world population had increased drastically since I was born. There were nine billion people in the world, five billion of them were in the United States, thirty million in New York, three million of them were here in Brooklyn, and one hundred and fifty thousand were right here in Division 12. The real scary statistic was our poverty level. Eighty-five percent of the United States was in poverty. That's four hundred and fifty billion of us completely dirt poor. The other fifteen percent, or fifty billion people, made up what we call the Elites. They were mostly government officials, politicians, and celebrities. They went to separate schools and lived in separate communities. The places where they lived weren't called Divisions; they were called Villages. The Elites had a special name for people like us who lived outside of their utopia.

Hoodlums.

The closest Elite Village to us was BK-Atlas. It was a completely private Village with its own housing and private school only for the Elite children. It wasn't far from us—about a twenty-minute walk, but the entire Village was gated and secured with a fifty-foot wall. They had their own grocery stores, theatres, shops, and sports arenas all inside the walls. For being so close, it might as well have been a world away.

We lived nothing like that, and the government made sure we could never get inside those gates. ID passes were used for everything around here from opening doors and entering buildings, to accessing bank accounts and redeeming our food ration tickets. For my family, we were lucky to each have our own room. Well, sort of. We converted the dining room into a room for Nana. It didn't have windows, but she said there was nothing to see out there anyway. I slept on the couch in the living room. It was the focal point of the apartment, and I did have a window. At night the moon shined brightly through the window, providing me with more than enough light to read a book or write in my journal.

I was switching off between two of my mother's books she had saved for me: *Anne of Green Gables* and *Little Women*. When I wasn't reading, I was writing in my journal about my thoughts, or sometimes stories. It was a release for me, and also a bit of an escape. However, I was lucky if I got a complete thought onto paper before beckoning calls from each corner of the apartment began at night.

Nana wanted someone to tell her stories to, and I loved to listen. Most of her stories were about her life growing up in the 1970s. Some were about a man she loved called Chuck Norris. Lou wanted to hear my stories, and secretly I knew she was scared of the dark.

Lou wasn't planned. Mom was forty when she had her. Lou had never heard sound, but she loved songs and stories all the same. She was born deaf so in our house sign language was used just as frequently as the spoken word.

Her favorite story was one I made up about a little mouse named Fox. Fox lived with all his little mouse brothers and sisters. At night they would go around the house and collect crumbs from the humans. When morning would come, and it was time for the little mice to go to sleep, Fox became scared that the food they gathered would be taken and that they would go hungry. So, he told all his brothers and sisters that they would have to work as a team to protect the Mouse House. The little mice would sleep back to back, with a mouse facing each direction so that they could be each other's lookout. That always made her fall asleep with a smile on her face.

Dad was always in need of help with something or another, whether it was his vid or phone. He was born in the 90s, so he was practically a dinosaur. And as for Theo—he hadn't called me to his room in a while.

Mom had worked as a teacher, but when the school budget was cut once again three years ago, she lost that position. Now the public schools consisted of a maximum one teacher per every fifty kids and all ages were mixed in the same classroom. I knew ten-year-olds who couldn't read.

It wasn't like that when my mom was there. Everyone loved her—she was warm and nurturing. Now she volunteers at the Rec Center tutoring kids and hosting craft nights. But don't let all the sweetness fool you. Lou might have been an angel, but raising my brother could have driven a saint mad. Plus, she kept my father and Nana in line, and that was no easy feat. She was an intricate combination of iron and silk.

A man wearing tattered beige pants and a straw hat playing the bongos on the sidewalk looked up at me. *God, is this man going to talk to me?*

"Hey, Scrubs!" he exclaimed in a singsong voice. He let out a light chuckle. "You're a nurse. Working for the man. That's cool, that's cool. I'm Mike. Nice hat. It's chill. Do you like mine? It's pure hemp."

I wondered if that was a question I was supposed to respond to or if he was just talking to himself. "Yes. It's nice," I finally replied, as I continued to walk past him.

"No, wait!" he called for me.

I blinked and turned my face toward him. He began talking before I made eye contact.

"I want you to know I'm cool with you being here. I'm cool with your people."

I stared at him for a moment puzzled by his declaration. "Okay," I said blankly. "Bye." *Please stop talking to me.* I turned to walk away once more.

"I'm all about equality, and I want you to know you're welcome here. The way I see it, we are one." He joined his hands together to symbolize that last word.

I looked around and wondered if he was really talking to me or just reciting a monologue. Just then a text message came through on my phone. It was my coworker, Lee:

Hurry in, El. Two of the lead doctors called out today, and it's getting crazy over here. No more beds.

Great.

"Well, I've got to get to work. Have a nice day," I managed to say it as kindly as I could. I even threw in a smile. I don't think I could have been more eager for the conversation to end. But it didn't.

"Wait, nurse lady! Let me give you something. Here is ... a seed. I got it out of my apple this morning. I have more. I save them all. When you get home plant it. You know everything in this world started as a seed.

A 'what-could-be.'" Mike was proudly holding the seed between his thumb and pointer finger at eye level as he gave this speech.

I was surprised that I agreed with him on his seed philosophy. I reached out my hand, and he placed the apple seed gently into my palm. "Thanks," I said, looking at the seed. "I'll be sure to plant this—I have just the place." I couldn't believe a sincere smile spread across my face when I took his leftover breakfast in my hand. His idea was quite nice. Maybe Mike and I had more in common than I originally thought.

"Nice! A farmer nurse ... I like it!" Mike yelled with a wide grin.

If he wasn't so self-righteous, he could be quite pleasant. I imagined what a friendship with a hipster would be like for a second as I turned to continue on my way. As I turned, I caught the gaze of two Elite women both wearing white pantsuits drinking what I could assume was their low-fat caramel macchiatos. They sat at an old picnic table that was in front of what used to be a private store. For some reason, I didn't think they had any apple seeds in their pockets.

They looked at me with menacing smirks. Something was creepy about them. Elites normally stayed out of the slums, but they made appearances every now and again. I think it made the hipsters feel accepted, but they always ran back behind their gates before night fell. The hipsters thought they were part of the Elites' class, but I guess they didn't notice they were stuck outside the walls with us.

Maybe it was something in the air today, but those two women sent a chill down my spine. They continued to watch me as I walked past. I had to cross the street to get to the stairs to my train platform. I looked both ways and saw no cars as usual. There were never many cars in the slums because driving was outlawed for citizens in the Divisions. Only government bureaucrats and residents of the Elite Villages were permitted to obtain drivers licenses as per a bill passed by the Torrent administration. They claimed it was for cleaner air. However, it didn't stop them from traveling in their private jets. As I stepped off the sidewalk into the street a Hummer limo came speeding around the corner, tires screeching, almost running me down. *What the hell!* I jumped back as the hummer continued to speed away. *Typical Elite.* I headed up the stairs to wait for my train. It should have been there already, but I guessed it would be coming soon. Train delays were another problem in the city. We were lucky to even have trains left. Out of the twenty-seven Subway lines that used to operate in NYC, only six remained in operation: the 1, 3, 7, D, N, and Q. All the rest were decommissioned almost a decade ago.

The four hundred or so entrances that led to the dormant lines were blocked off, and many of the tunnels themselves crumbled without maintenance and upkeep. Even if a track was intact, it was best to avoid the abandoned stations. The displaced and disposed had found their way down there along with the ill, convicts, and addicts. Even the gangsters didn't go down there. The BK12 built their fortresses in abandoned buildings and old water treatment facilities above ground.

Five minutes passed. Nothing. *Huh.*

I heard my phone ring thinking it would be my coworker, Lee, asking where I was, but it was my dad. I answered but before I could even say 'hello' he was talking.

"El, get Lou. Do not let her get on the bus. Get home and lock the doors. Your mother and I will be home soon!"

Before I could respond, the line cut out. I looked down at my phone. No bars. It wasn't exactly atypical to have a conversation cut short like that. The cell towers weren't too dependable considering there was only one provider who was—you guessed it—the government.

My father's words processed in my head. I looked up at where the two women were sitting just a moment ago, but now just their two cups of coffee remained on the table. Mike was still playing his bongos. I decided to head down the stairs. A loud sound from above me brought my attention to the sky where an airplane flew close overhead.

Then two of them.

Then another.

They didn't look like commercial planes, rather they were smaller and had what appeared to be military markings on the wings. I began to see some more people complaining that their phones weren't working. With so few towers operating and so few workers to repair operating one's outages were to be expected.

But my father's frantic words still played loudly in my head. I started to head back to my apartment. In the distance, I saw a big yellow bus. It was Lou's bus pulling up in front of our-building four blocks away, and there was Lou with her backpack heading toward it.

"Lou! Lou!" I waved my hands in the air and ran toward her, trying to get her attention. "Wait!" I hollered, hoping her bus driver would hear me.

She was already on the first step of the bus when Theo came around the back end of it and scooped her into his arms. I watched him tell the bus driver something and then the driver closed the doors and drove away. I met up with them in front of the building out of breath and thankful.

"Did you get a call from Dad?" Theo asked.

"Yeah," I breathed heavily. "Let's get inside," I said with a glance up and down the street. I put a hand on his back as we hurried inside the building. We jogged up the stairs to the second floor and into our apartment, locking the door behind us as we were told to, still unsure what exactly was happening.

Nana was on the couch looking through my diary.

"Oh, I thought you had left for the day," she said, startled as she closed the book and tucked it back under the sofa cushion. I had caught her reading it once before, but I couldn't bring myself to be angry with her. It wasn't like she had anything better to do in the apartment all day.

We tried calling our parents, but the lines were still jammed up. Theo turned on the vid. He switched to a news station. The Brooklyn Bridge was closed in both directions due to an accident.

Strange.

Since driving was outlawed for most people, there weren't many cars on the road other than an occasional government official or traveling Elite. Although there were people within the Divisions that had cars stored away secretly, it didn't sit well with me that all six lanes of the bridge were closed. The subways and trains reported closures and delays also. That explained why my train never came. Theo switched around and checked multiple stations. All of them announced the same three things.

Multiple bridge closures. Extensive train delays. Downed cell towers. One news anchor joked, "I remember cell service went down on New Year's Eve last year. I couldn't wish my mother a Happy New Year!" The anchor laughed an unnatural laugh showing all of his overly whitened teeth. We sat impatiently around the apartment for twenty minutes until Mom and Dad busted through the door.

"I need you three to get to the basement!" Dad exclaimed before we could say a word.

Suddenly I heard the anchor say there was breaking news. "This just in ... there seems to be a situation over in Detroit and a similar situation in Chicago of a bomb releasing some sort of gas into the atmosphere." Then the station went into static.

Dad had two gas masks in his hand. He was running around the apartment throwing blankets, towels, and tools into a large black garbage bag. Mom was collecting Nana's medicines.

"What's going on, Dad?" I asked.

"War! El, I need you to get your sister and brother down to the basement now. Your mother will take Nana."

"War? What do you mean?" I asked in disbelief. Certainly, he didn't mean actual war.

"We don't have much time," explained Dad, rushing to the kitchen and loading food into the large bag.

"What about everyone else?" I cried.

Dad didn't miss a beat. "I'll handle that. You go and don't stop for anything."

"Dad, I can help!" Theo pleaded.

Dad ignored him.

"Who's attacking us?" I asked. I fully knew by my father's tone that it wasn't the time for questions, but I couldn't set aside the need to understand what was happening.

"Don't worry about that now," Dad yelled. "We don't have time to talk … we have minutes, maybe seconds."

"Dad?" Theo pleaded again. "I'll help gather the neighbors, okay?"

"No, Theo! Go downstairs with your sisters!" Dad bellowed as he spun around to stare him directly in the eyes. "There are two large jugs of water on the first landing. Grab them on your way down."

"The news said bomb. Should we get out of the city?" I asked. My brow furrowed with questions.

"And go where El?" Dad yelled. "The bridges are closed and so is the subway. Even if they weren't, where would we go? Your grandmother's house? We don't have the means to get out of the city. The bomb is going to hit any second. Now, what did I tell you? Go down to the basement and stop for nothing and nobody!"

Both Theo and I knew we shouldn't argue the situation any further. I took Lou by the hand and Theo followed right behind us as we headed out of the apartment. As we entered the hallway, my neighbor Kai opened his door.

"El?" Kai asked. He must have heard the screaming.

"Kai, we have to get your grandfather and hurry downstairs. Something is happening."

Kai read the urgent expression on my face and didn't ask questions.

"Okay. We'll meet you down there."

"I'll help you," I told him as I took a step forward.

"No," Kai said sternly. "Go El. We'll meet you down there."

"No. I'm helping you," I repeated. Kai was my best friend and leaving him behind hadn't crossed my mind. "Theo, take Lou."

"No. No matter what happens get your sister and yourself to where your father told you to go. I will be down there. I promise," Kai assured me.

I didn't want to leave without him, but I knew Kai, and I knew he wouldn't let me win this argument. Time would be wasted squabbling. Dad's scream was still ringing in my ears.

"Hurry, then," I said to him, grabbing Lou's hand tight and continuing for the stairs. As we descended the first flight, I heard Dad run into the hallway and up a flight to the fourth floor. I could hear him pounding on the doors as his scream echoed through the building. I had heard that scream before.

When Theo was thirteen, he got into a fight with a neighboring gang down by our park. He wound up getting stabbed six times in his side and back, puncturing his lungs. One of Theo's friends came to our apartment to tell us what had happened, and my father ran down to the park. He pulled Theo into his arms and started running toward the hospital. The way he screamed at Theo to just hold on was the way he was yelling for the neighbors to come downstairs.

We hurried down the steps, rounding each landing and continuing to the next but stopped in our tracks when we saw a body lying face down on the first-floor landing.

"Shit, is that Mrs. Carter?" Theo exclaimed.

"She must have fallen!" I cried running over to her.

Theo and Lou held their positions while I approached her quickly at first, and then more cautiously as I remembered my father's words. "Mrs. Carter?" I whispered, reaching out a hand to touch her shoulder. "Mrs. Carter?" I leaned in and turned her body slightly. Her eyes were wide open and still. A trail of blood leaked from her nose and down the side of her mouth. I gasped. She was dead.

Lou screamed.

"Let's go," I ordered vehemently, grabbing Lou by the hand and speeding down the stairs.

I took note of the blood on Mrs. Carter and the lack of blood on the ground. *It didn't appear to be a fall that killed her.*

She must have had a stroke or an aneurysm and perhaps hit the ground softly because I didn't notice any bruises on her head or hands. I had to stop myself from thinking about the details much further. All I knew was that she was dead, and from what Dad was saying we would be too if we didn't get downstairs quickly. We continued to run down the stairs until we hit the ground floor. As we rounded the corner to go to the basement level, I heard someone bang on the glass. It was Emily, and she was knocking on the front door. I took half a step to let her in then I stopped.

She wasn't knocking.

She was walking into the glass over and over. My eyes narrowed. I stayed frozen, staring, while my brain tried to process what I was seeing. She was bleeding from her nose, mouth, and head.

Just then, Dad, Mom, and Nan ran up behind us along with Kai and his grandfather. Kai took my hand. Dad grabbed a water jug, and Theo grabbed the other.

"Where are Rose and Mr. Carter?" I asked.

Dad pushed us forward as he glanced back.

"Let's go!"

When we reached the basement, we saw the Adersons already there. It wasn't until Dad locked the doors that I thought about the hospital.

Chapter Three

Dad said Mr. Carter had been with them. Our only guess was that he must have stopped following them when he saw his wife's body on the first-floor landing. We hadn't heard or felt a bomb. This attack was something else, but we couldn't be certain what it was. So, we all sat in silence. Joined together by our ignorance.

Our building's basement was designated as a fallout shelter during the Cold War. It was one of forty thousand or so in the city. Most buildings redesigned the space into laundry rooms or gyms after nuclear weapons were thought to no longer be an imminent threat. Ours seemed to be nothing more than empty, windowless space. We all sat in silence not knowing what to say. We all wondered the same thing. *What just happened and how long do we have to stay down here?*

Kai sat close to me. "You okay?" he asked, his eyes searching my face. They seemed to zero in on a small cut on my lip.

"Yeah, I'm fine," I lied as I licked the blood from my mouth.

"But what about the rest of the people in the building? Rose? Emma?" My gaze wasn't on any one person, and I'm not sure who I was asking the question to exactly, but my father responded.

"It's too late."

Kai and I both looked at Dad, startled by his sharp tone. "We can't open this door. Not for two weeks at least." Dad's voice was authoritative and stern. I could tell there was no arguing with him.

Ten days or two weeks Dad said was standard for the fallout levels to drop to one percent and then we can go upstairs to the apartments and look for survivors. He said that until then there was no leaving the shelter. My stomach ached at the thought. The first two days I didn't sleep at all. On day three everything became hazy down in that basement. We had light down there and the building's electricity surprisingly never gave out. There was enough canned food and water, but the smell was vile. Dad sectioned off the far-right corner of the room with trash bags and a bucket for personal use. The stench was intolerable. I perched myself high on the concrete stairs by the exit as far away from that corner as possible.

I was slumped over with my face in my hands, my elbows resting on my knees, completely lost in my own thoughts when Kai came over and sat next to me.

"What are you thinking about?" His voice was quiet and even.

I barely heard him. There was a ringing in my ears that seemed to be getting louder and louder.

"El?" His voice sharpened as he struggled to maintain a whisper. Sound traveled down in that basement.

I shook my head lightly and blinked my eyes, bringing myself back to reality. He was staring at me with concern.

"Sorry, Kai. I'm out of it," I replied, glancing at him briefly then looking away.

"There's nothing for you to be sorry about." Kai let those words linger in the air. His eyes stayed locked on mine.

I always forgot just how good-looking Kai was when we weren't together. Sitting next to him then reminded me. His light eyes and perfectly chiseled features were tense from the situation. I remembered his initial question. I sat up slightly and sighed. "I'm thinking about the hospital. The patients mostly, and the staff too. There's an air filtration system there but if the windows weren't sealed …" my words and gaze trailed off.

Kai's eyes moved to the ground in front of him. "I see," he said, holding this position. "You know there is a chance they survived. It's summer, and it was hot outside the day of the strike, so the air-conditioning was probably running with the windows closed. The hospital has a generator, plus like you said, they have the air filtration system." He looked back at me. Kai had a good point. He reached his arm over and touched my knee. It instantly comforted me. "We survived. That means others must have, too," he added.

"We don't know if we survived, yet," I muttered. I leaned my head onto his shoulder. His touch eased me. Kai was always helping me get through tough situations. Over the years we went from being neighbors to friends to more than friends. And now, finally, we are best friends. I wouldn't give up our status as best friends for anything.

When we were sixteen and seniors in high school, we went on our one and only school trip to the Rations Center. It was as fun as it sounds. I got separated from the group in the building when I stopped to read a poster about the government issued aptitude test—the test my father failed and the reason for his unemployment. When I couldn't find my class, I walked outside the nearest exit thinking I would wait by the school bus until they returned. There wasn't anything I was interested in seeing in the Rations Center anyway. But I exited on the wrong side of the building. I was on the far west side instead of the north. I figured I would just walk around, but what I didn't realize was that the alley behind the Rations Center had become a hangout for degenerates.

A drunken man from across the street noticed me and saw that I was alone. When he started heckling me, I turned around and tried to get back into the building, but it was locked from the inside. He noticed I was locked out.

I began walking faster to get to the other side of the building where the bus must have parked. When I turned back the man had begun following me. I heard him say something about taking me home. Just then a door opened a few yards ahead of me. Kai stepped out. The man stopped in his tracks.

Kai had always looked like an Elite. His good looks and clothing, along with his demeanor and comportment just radiated ELITE. This helped him in ways he couldn't even understand—people didn't mess with the Elite.

"El!" he called for me as he closed the distance between us with a slight jog. "I was looking for you. I saw you go outside."

"Hey." I turned around to make sure the man had left. He had. I looked back at Kai. "I was just getting some fresh air and the door shut behind me," I lied. I didn't want him to know how stupid I was to come outside alone in this area.

"You could have told me. I would have come outside with you," he insisted. I let the conversation end there.

"Let's go inside," I said grabbing him by the arm as we walked together around to the front of the warehouse.

We kissed one summer down by the river, but it was a one-time thing. Kai could have had any girl he wanted. Even some of the Elite girls liked him, and I wasn't interested in competing for a guy. More than that, I wasn't willing to give Kai up as a friend. I loved him and the thought of us being together, breaking up, and not being friends anymore hurt worse than us never being more than friends. I needed him to be my best friend because I wasn't fully me without him by my side. This didn't mean I wasn't attracted to him—I was. His very presence made me feel like a fifteen-year-old girl with her first crush, but I had plans for medical school, and I knew that coursework would take up most of my time anyway.

I began going in and out of consciousness. It was day three, and we still had at least seven days to go in the shelter. Lou had slept most of the day. Something seemed wrong.

"Dad, it doesn't feel like there is any air down here," I swallowed hard and took a deep breath, but it didn't satisfy.

My father looked unfazed. He was fiddling with the filtration system. "The flue is blocked. It's letting in a small amount of air, but it's not enough to sustain us for another week."

"How do we open it?" Mr. Aderson asked.

"It's not a matter of just opening it," Dad said. "We have to make sure the filtration system is intact when we start the fan or else we will just be letting in contaminated air."

"The roof," Mom said. "That is where the access to the main vent system is."

"Yes," Dad replied. "The vent is on the roof. We will need to clear the flue from the fourth floor."

"So, two of us can go up and clean out of the vents and open the flue while one person down here makes sure the filtration system stays intact," Mr. Aderson said.

"I can go with you, Mr. Logan," Kai offered, as he stood, pushing up the sleeves of his shirt.

"No, Kai. It isn't physical strength that we need. We need someone small enough to fit in the spaces down the flue if the clog is lower than we expect," Dad said.

"You and I will go." My mother's voice was soft but significant. She was five-foot-three, and besides Lou, she was the smallest person in the shelter. "Paul will stay here and see to it that the filtration is working. If anything should go wrong shut the flue immediately."

My mom and dad put on the gas masks and left. Mr. Aderson took post at the vent while Theo, Kai, and I waited anxiously by the stairwell. Approximately thirty minutes later, Dad came rushing in with Mr. Carter in one arm, and Mom wrapped in the other. Dad collapsed to the floor, and I ran over to him

"Your mother," Dad gasped. He was out of breath.

I turned Mom over onto her side.

"Mom!" Theo ran over to her. "Are you okay?"

I was looking for answers in her eyes because she wasn't responding. They were open, but she wasn't looking at anything. I glanced down at her hands.

"I love you," she signed and closed her eyes.

"Mom!" I screamed. I turned her onto her back and began administering CPR.

"Dad, we have to get her to the hospital!" I yelled.

For a man with no breath, my father screamed loud. It was the sound of a broken heart. Theo held Lou, and Kai kneeled behind me. I pressed on her chest in repetition, and then breathed into her lungs. I continued this for ten minutes. During those minutes the world simply stopped. And then I had to stop, too.

Dad crawled over to my mother and held her body for what seemed like an eternity. Mrs. Aderson took the mask off Mr. Carter and applied water to his face with a rag. She also placed a blanket over my mother.

Four hours later my father told us what had happened. Mom and Dad ascended to the fourth floor. The flue was clogged just like Dad suspected it would be. Mom climbed in and cleared it. When they headed to the roof to check on the exhaust system, they saw Mr. Carter. He was sitting on a chair inside the greenhouse. The door was closed. No one else from the apartment survived.

"Mr. Carter? When did you get up here?" Dad asked through the glass.

Mr. Carter didn't respond right away.

"Mr. Carter?" Dad repeated.

Mr. Carter looked up. He seemed relieved to see that my parents were okay, but he was still so evidently heartbroken. "My wife," he strained to whisper. His speech was garbled, and it was difficult to tell if that strain came from dehydration or heartbreak. "I laid her down over there." He pointed to the rose garden. Mrs. Carter's foot was exposed amidst the brush.

"Mr. Carter, come downstairs with us. We have medical supplies and water," Dad said.

"The air isn't safe, Logan. Look. No birds. No squirrels. Not even a rat." Mr. Carter struggled to speak. His speech was slurred and muffled.

He was right, however. Something was wrong. The air must have still been contaminated, or else animals would have come out of hiding.

"Mr. Carter, can you hold your breath while we get you inside?" Mom asked.

Mr. Carter was clearly disoriented. He began to sob. Both of my parents knew he wouldn't be able to hold his breath.

"Mr. Carter, it's going to be okay," Mom said reassuringly. Mom had looked directly at my father as she spoke. "Mr. Carter, I'm going to give you my mask."

It didn't take long for my dad to interrupt. "No, Helen," he exclaimed as he reached out and grasped her wrist.

"Yes, Curtis," my mom said softly now looking at Mr. Carter. "You know, I was captain of my high school swim team. I'm able to hold my breath ... for two and a half minutes to be exact."

Dad held tight to Mom's wrist. "We will go down to the shelter together, and you'll stay down there while I come back up with your mask for him. No one has to hold their breath," Dad argued.

Mom looked over at Mr. Carter. "His breathing is shallow, and he is disoriented, Curtis. There's no time. We can't leave him up here. We are lucky he made it this long."

My father was still not convinced.

"There's no other way," Mom continued. "I know the type of man you are ... you don't leave people behind."

She always knew just what to say to get her way. It was part of the reason Dad fell in love with her. Her endless optimism.

"Okay. Let's do this quickly." Dad released Mom's wrist. "I'll take Mr. Carter downstairs. You just get back to the shelter quickly."

Mom removed her mask and handed it to my father.

"Go!" Dad demanded, motioning for her to run.

Mom headed into the building swiftly as Dad watched her. He stared at the building for a few more seconds and then turned back to the greenhouse. He approached the zipper. "Okay, Mr. Carter, hold your breath for me on the count of one, two, three." Dad opened the door. As quickly as he could, he put the mask on Mr. Carter.

Due to the shallowness of his breathing, it wouldn't have mattered anyhow—he wasn't getting much oxygen in his lungs either way without his inhaler. That is possibly what had saved him to begin with.

"There we go," Dad said as he secured the mask on tightly. "Now, let's get downstairs." My dad used all his strength to lift Mr. Carter's one hundred and thirty pounds up off the chair. Dad looked up and saw my mom through his struggle. "Helen! Go downstairs now! That was the deal."

My mother just stood there.

"Helen?" he repeated. In the doorway behind my mom stood Rose, covered in blood holding Emma in her arms seemingly in a trance.

"Go, Helen. Now. Get to the shelter!" The words were muffled through the mask, but Mom didn't budge. The gas seemed to affect people differently. The best my father could guess was that my mother gasped when she saw Rose and Emma, causing her to breathe the gas into her lungs. Killing her.

We made sure Mr. Carter took in plenty of fluids as he stayed in bed for the following days. When he started to feel better, he began asking about my mom, but we didn't tell him. He would have felt like it was his fault and I didn't want him to bear that burden. Not right now.

I saw the pain in my dad's eyes as we took my mother to the roof and laid her body down in the rose garden next to Mrs. Carter. I laid myself down next to my mother for the last time and wept on her chest. I could have stayed there forever. I felt my father's hand on my shoulder, and with tears in his eyes, he helped me to my feet. It was unclear how my family would go on without my mother since she was our glue. I could tell my father was thinking the same thing. We locked the roof so that no one could get up there. The next few days passed like a bad dream.

On the tenth day, I told my dad that I couldn't take it anymore. I had to get out. I was literally going to lose my mind. I promised to stay within the building, but he still said "no." Three days earlier, Dad and Mr. Aderson had gone up to the roof to look for signs of life. They said they saw people walking about, but they looked sick and infected. Some of the ill were running wildly through the street attempting to get into buildings.

Dad and Mr. Aderson had searched the building for survivors but found none. They did find supplies, and then they secured the entries and exits to the building. They had been going up and emptying the waste bucket multiple times a day, so I knew it was safe at least within the building. I urged my father once more.

"Dad, please. I need to see sunlight even if it's through the glass. I'll keep the mask on, and I'll stay right on the ground floor." I stared up at my father.

He was cleaning the air filtration system, so he didn't even look up to say "no."

Kai joined me at my side. "I'll go with her, Mr. Logan. I won't let anything happen to her," he said.

My father paused what he was doing and looked at us both. "Thirty minutes. Don't be late." He went back to cleaning the filters.

The gas mask felt strange, like a heavy weight on your face that you had to hold up using neck muscles you didn't even know you had. It looked just as strange as it felt—like an alien pig creature with a long snout and one large eye centered in the middle of its face.

When we reached the ground floor, I continued to head toward the stairs to go up to the first floor. We would have to go out one of the windows from there because the ground floor windows were boarded up, along with the front and side doors. I turned back to Kai, remembering I hadn't yet told him of my plan.

"I'm going to the hospital," I said, as I started up the stairs. I was headed toward Emily and Russ's apartment. I knew that apartment well. We could leave from their kitchen window.

"What? No, El." Kai's voice sounded sturdy, although muffled through the mask. He may not have known my plan to sneak over to the hospital, but I knew he would come with me. He would come because he wouldn't want me to go alone and that was his weakness that I intended to take advantage of.

"I told your dad I would make sure nothing happened to you," he exclaimed.

"I know. That's why you're coming with me." I smiled even though I knew he couldn't see it.

Leaving the shelter was like waking up out of a nightmare. It was relief combined with terror. I waited for Kai to acknowledge what I already knew. We were going.

"El, it's not a good idea. We don't even know what's out there," he responded quickly.

"You're the one who said it yourself," I responded just as quickly. "There could be survivors, and if there are, they need medical help."

He didn't move. I guessed he still wasn't convinced.

"I'm going with or without you," I said, turning to walk away. I didn't enjoy giving him an ultimatum, but I wasn't changing my mind. I was a nurse, and I *had* to save people.

I reached the first floor and headed down the hallway approaching Emily and Russ' door. I heard Kai's footsteps behind me and smiled. I twisted the doorknob, gave the door a push, and let it swing open. It opened to their kitchen, and Kai and I stepped inside. We looked around. Everything seemed to be in order. Their cat Shelby walked by casually giving us a *meow* and nothing else.

Kai and I shot each other an uneasy look. We walked through the kitchen and toward the living room where the fire escape was. I opened the window, and without hesitation, I climbed out. Kai followed right behind me.

"We have thirty minutes to get there and back. We need transportation," Kai said, jumping to the ground beside me.

I had landed roughly and was getting up off the ground and wiping the dirt off my hands as he spoke. Kai knew where some of the neighbor kids stored their bikes. Lucky for us they were still there propped up against the stone wall in the alleyway between our apartment building and the next. We each took a bike and headed down the road.

The streets were covered in carnage. It was worse than what Dad had described. Bodies lay on top of one another scattered across the sidewalks and street. An occasional car was crashed up on the sidewalk. Blood ran down the side of the street into the drain like rain. Some spots were so heavily compacted with debris that we had to dismount from our bikes and walk them through while some avenues were completely clear of bodies altogether.

As we approached the corner of our street, I spotted Mike. It was like he was frozen in time sitting crossed legged on the ground same as the last time I saw him, only now he was slumped over his bongos. His eyes were wide open, and his head hung down inches from the pavement. His hat laid flat on the ground under his head.

It didn't make sense, and we didn't have enough information to theorize why this was. But it struck us as odd. The one and only thing I was thankful for at that moment was the fact that the smell didn't permeate through the mask.

It took eleven minutes to reach the hospital on bike—longer than we had expected with so many of the roads being blocked. We walked in. It seemed just as eerily vacant inside. The gift store was in front of us.

"We don't have a lot of time. We have six minutes to get what we need, find and treat any survivors, and get out of here," I said. "There are vending machines by the cafeteria. Why don't you go get some sodas and snacks—we'll tell Dad we got them from the apartments. I'll go to the nurse's station and get supplies."

Kai insisted on coming with me, but I reasoned with him to get snacks. It would heighten the morale of the neighbors in the shelter, and they could all use the boost. He knew I was right. I told him to keep an eye out for any survivors.

Kai reluctantly took an "I Love NY" canvas backpack from the gift shop and headed toward the vending machines. I turned in the other direction to the stairs going up to the second floor toward the nurse's station.

It was quiet aside from the hum of the lights. I heard glass shatter from down the hall. I shook my head thinking of Kai stealing candy bars—guess he wasn't such a goody two shoes after all. I reached the second-floor landing and walked through the doors into the hallway. As I walked, I peeked into some of the rooms. They were empty. Papers were scattered, and things were out of place, but there wasn't a single person, or body, in sight.

Could all the patients have been evacuated?

I neared the nurse's station and looked at my desk. A photo of Lou, Theo and me from three summers ago at Lou's fourth birthday party was right where I had left it, taped to the corner of my station next to my computer portal. Portals were the modern version of the old school computer. Upon looking at it, you wouldn't think it was anything special. It was a long, slender, rectangular slab of hard plastic that resembled a ruler. However, a wave of the hand over the portal would activate a virtual keyboard and screen. I ripped off the picture. Lou had her face painted as a clown, and Theo was holding her in his arms while I held her cake with the four lit candles.

I remembered the day like it happened yesterday. Mom had been the one to take the picture. She saved up so much money from her teaching job to buy the paint, the cake, and the piñata. She filled it with all of Lou's favorite candies. I wondered how our lives would be changed now without her.

Suddenly I heard a noise. It sounded like it was coming from the medical supply closet down the hall and to the left. I put the photo in my pocket and headed toward the closet. I heard another crash from within. I paused and peered inside cautiously.

There was a man. He wasn't wearing a mask. He was rummaging through the medical supplies. My initial thought was perhaps he was a drug addict looking for medications, but that was the world before the gas attack. Now I thought maybe he was just a survivor like me. I studied him from behind. He didn't look like a patient or a doctor. He looked like a soldier. I didn't think I had made a noise, but he spun around and pointed a knife at me. I instinctively put both of my hands up.

"It's okay! I'm a nurse," I announced quickly. I stood frozen while I watched for his reaction. His fierce eyes softened just slightly, and he relaxed his posture.

"Where'd you come from?" he asked, surprising me with how even his tone was.

"My family and I live a few blocks away. We survived in our building's fallout shelter." I stopped there. I didn't want to give him too much information.

He looked at me for a long moment then spoke. "What are you doing here?" he asked.

"I'm looking for survivors. Like I said, I'm a nurse," I repeated. That's when I noticed the blood on his jacket. "You're bleeding." I went over to take a closer look. There was a large bloodstain on his denim jacket and a huge gash in the fabric that exposed his split forearm.

He pulled away. "I'm fine," he said roughly.

"You need stitches," I said.

"I don't need help. I'll be fine," he insisted.

"Please," I begged. I guess it was the fact that he was the only survivor I found and maybe I was determined to at least help someone. Maybe it was because I couldn't save my mother. Perhaps I needed to help him more than he needed the help itself, but I grabbed his arm and inspected the wound. It was filthy. I reached for antiseptic and a cotton ball. It was convenient that we were already in the supply room.

"Please. Come with me," I said, taking him by the wrist into the nearest room with a bed. I had him sit down so I could prep his wound for stitches. "What's your name?" I asked.

He looked out the window and down the hall like he was looking for someone.

"Are you alone?" I asked.

"Pratt," he answered.

I guessed that Pratt was his name and that he had answered my first question. I was about to ask the second question again, but I studied him instead. Pratt. He was handsome. He was tall with an athletic build. His dark brown hair came into a widow's peak, and his eyebrows seemed naturally raised with concern. I wonder how many years of worrying had imprinted that look on him. His broad shoulders pulled a black shirt tight across his chest and a denim jacket over that. The denim was torn, but he was lucky to have been wearing it. I imagined it absorbed some of the impact from whatever had cut him.

He took off the jacket as he told me he was from Division 4—the Brooklyn bridge section of the city. He continued to tell me that he was just out gathering supplies. I wondered why he came all the way to this hospital considering there were two others in closer Divisions, but I didn't ask.

"How do you know the air isn't contaminated?" I asked.

"I'm alive, aren't I?" he responded. He had a point.

I had finished cleaning the wound and was about to begin stitching. The needle was proving difficult to handle with the mask obstructing my peripheral vision. To look even slightly to one side required me to move my entire head. I wasn't going to be able to stitch like that. I took off my mask and placed it on the table at my side.

I inhaled once and paused.

I exhaled. "This may sting a bit," I warned him, but he didn't flinch. I proceeded to stitch. He told me there weren't any survivors in the hospital. He said that he'd already looked through the Division's hospitals and Rations Center and hadn't found any survivors.

"My father said that he had seen people walking," I said.

"They're not alive," Pratt said.

I stopped stitching and looked up at him, but I didn't speak. "The gas was some sort of sleeping agent," he began. "It killed a lot of people, but it didn't kill some all the way. Their bodies I mean. Or at least that's what I think."

I tried to process his theory. "Then where are all the patients who were here in the hospital?" I asked.

"Maybe they were evacuated," he answered.

"No. Not these people. We don't have the means for that," I responded.

"Maybe their bodies all walked away after inhaling the gas," he tried.

Unlikely. From his lack of eye contact and his fidgeting leg, it appeared he didn't even believe his own theory.

"It's irreversible," Pratt said matter-of-factly. He held his jaw tight, and his narrow eyes darted to the doorway. I turned around to see if anyone was there. There wasn't. But it still seemed like he was looking for someone. I continued to stitch, but I was listening to his words carefully. He seemed to know much more than we did.

"The gas' effect. It can't be undone ... they're just dead people walking," he continued.

I looked him in the eyes and then back down at his arm. "That can't be true," I said. But I didn't know if I believed my own words.

I finished the last stitch and cut the string. Then I began cleaning up the wrappers and supplies as pointless as that seemed. All my patients were gone, and so was my city from what I could tell. "I'll tell my family that it's safe to come out now. We can—" I started, but before I could finish my sentence Pratt interjected.

"Wait one more day," he said sternly. He pointed to the sky. "The fallout is almost settled, but any slight breeze will stir it up. It's supposed to rain tonight. One more day will wash the residue away."

"How is it that you know all of this?" I asked him.

Suddenly Kai busted through the door. "El, get back!" Kai leaped between Pratt and me, not hesitating for a second. Pratt jumped up.

Good thing I had finished stitching.

Kai was in a fighting stance with his fists up, jaw clenched.

"Kai, it's fine!" I shouted, putting a hand on his arm to bring it down. "He's a survivor like us. He was injured looking for supplies. I gave him a few stitches."

Kai looked down at Pratt's arm. His stance softened only slightly. "Put your mask on El," Kai muffled through his mask without taking his eyes off Pratt.

I opened my mouth to tell Kai that we didn't need our masks when Pratt interrupted.

"You should put your mask back on," Pratt said. He held up one finger. "One more day then maybe we will hear some announcements." He shot a quick look up and down at Kai. I assumed he was assessing whether he could have taken him. By the small smirk that settled on Pratt's face, I think he assumed yes.

"If I were you, I wouldn't mention that you had your mask off or that you met me. People will hear that sort of thing, and they'll try to make a run for it. It isn't safe," he added.

I thought of all the neighbors in the shelter. He was right that they would run out of there like bats out of hell and who would blame them? Pratt grabbed his jacket off the bed and turned to leave. He hesitated at the door.

"I would keep off the main street," he warned us.

Before we could ask why he was gone. Kai and I left right behind him, but Pratt had disappeared into the streets before I could see which way he headed. I stopped and looked around for a moment.

"Let's go," Kai said. Kai was right. We didn't have time to spare.

We jumped on our bikes and headed back home taking the side roads. They were mostly clear, and the ride took us eight minutes—much faster than the ride to the hospital. We dropped the bikes down in the back alley and rushed back downstairs to the shelter, fifteen minutes late.

Dad was still working on the filtration system when we got downstairs. He shot us a stern look and turned away. I guess he figured we'd been through enough and spared us the lecture.

We handed out the vending machine treats to the neighbors, and Kai gave Lou a teddy bear he gotten from the gift shop especially for her.

The following morning at five. we were awoken by the sound of helicopters and President Torrent's voice on the ividcam. My father and Mr. Aderson grabbed gas masks and ran up to see what was going on. We waited down below for them to return. Dad seemed shocked when he came downstairs. He took off the mask and told us it was over.

If he only knew how accurate those words were. I wondered how Pratt had known all of this.

Chapter Four

The relief of being out of the shelter didn't last long.

The ividcam was playing on repeat: "Please convene at your local Rations Center."

We were tired and anxious, dehydrated and hungry. But mostly, we wanted answers. The main street that was cluttered with death yesterday was now almost completely clear of bodies other than a few scattered in the brush and in the parks. The evidence of the carnage, however, was still apparent. There was the stench of death in the air. Smog and debris flew in the wind, and red stains streaked the roads and buildings.

We gathered at the Rations Center where the military tallied the numbers of survivors. It looked like there were no more than five hundred people in the Center altogether. Some people were asleep, and some were pacing around anxiously. There was water and bread with turkey and ham placed out for us on a row of tables. I had only eaten a cup of beans in the last three days, but I was surprisingly not hungry. A group of about thirty people were at the table making themselves sandwiches. I walked over to the table, pouring a cup of water and drinking it quickly. I filled up the cup again and headed back to my group.

"Here," I said, handing Mr. Carter the cup. "Drink some water." His hand was shaking as he grasped the cup and took a sip. I was glad he did. I watched him and thought about my mother and how I couldn't save her. I thought about how Mr. Carter was going to feel responsible for her death. It was too much to think about, so I stood up and turned away.

The security team was based in front of the locked crates of supplies. Theo was giving Nan her medicine. Lou was eating a piece of bread. Mrs. Aderson was holding a damp cloth on Kai's grandfather's head. Kai was with Mr. Aderson and my father, who were trying to get answers from one of the security officers.

"What's going on? Who attacked us? Don't you know anything?" my father asked.

The security officer didn't respond. My dad was becoming irritated, that much was clear.

"Where is Caleb?" I heard Dad ask about his old army friend who had worked at the Rations Center. A small group of people came walking through the door. I noticed Lee among them.

"Lee!" I called out to him. I ran over to him and embraced him tightly. "I'm so happy you're okay!" I cried, still hugging him.

"I can't believe I'm seeing you," he said. "How did you survive? You were on your way to work, weren't you?" Lee asked.

"I was. But ..." I didn't want to dive into the details of how my father was warned about the attack. "I left something at home and went back there to get it. We locked ourselves in the fallout shelter in our building's basement."

Lee looked over my shoulder to see who I meant by *we*.

"Your family made it too?" he asked, smiling. "That's great, El." His lips tightened as he tried to smile. Without words, I knew that his family didn't make it.

"I'm so sorry," I said. I knew the words weren't enough.

"I went home to find them, but they weren't there," he said, sighing as a tear streaked down his cheek. I embraced him tightly.

"You were at the hospital when it happened," I said, remembering the text I received from him the day of the attack.

"Yes. A few of the techs and I were in the basement getting more beds when it happened." He stopped talking. I followed his gaze to the front door.

A man in military uniform walked into the building. More soldiers came in behind him, and we watched as they made their way to the middle of the room. The man who appeared to be the leader stopped in the center, and the other soldiers lined up in rows to each side of him.

"Good morning, citizens. I am Colonel Yucon, Division 12's Martial Officer until further notice. First, I would like to say congratulations and job well done. You survived the un-survivable. We have plenty of food, water, and medical supplies. You will all be examined and treated by a doctor. Second, I know you all have some questions, and I want to fill you in. However, we are still a little fuzzy on the details. Now, my men and I have been cleaning the streets since last Tuesday. We have tried to clear out the bodies and the rubbish, but you may still come across some areas with left over ... causalities. You are by no means to interact with any person or persons who appear to be sleepwalking. This seems to be a side effect of the gas attack. If you are unsure, you can call us, and we will come assess the situation." Yucon looked over the crowd.

"You will have noticed a smell and smog in the air. We are burning the casualties to avoid contamination. You are to stay away from the burn centers. I know you want more answers and you'll get them. Tonight, President Torrent is to address the nation on the ividcam at seven p.m. Now until then you are welcome to eat, rest, hell, grab a pack of smokes and some beer, whatever you need. The doctor will be in shortly, and then you can head to your homes after being seen."

The shouted questions from the survivors went unanswered. The colonel ordered the Rations Center security team to unlock the gates. As soon as that happened people raced over to the shelves and began to collect items to take home.

I didn't move. I kept my eyes on the colonel. He looked down at his phone and brought it to his ear. I heard him speak, "Yeah, we have 546 here. The doctor hasn't seen them yet."

After seeing the doctor, everyone in our group went home except Mr. Maxwell. The doctors wanted him to stay overnight at the hospital. I offered to stay and work, but I was told that under the martial law for the next few days no civilian nurses could work at the hospital. Kai stayed behind to be with his grandfather a little longer. We carried supplies from the warehouse to our apartment. Walking into the apartment was bittersweet. To be home and out of the shelter was a relief, but looking at Rose's apartment door made my lip quiver. We headed upstairs and unpacked the food, waters, and linens that we had taken from the Rations Center.

At seven p.m. and we heard the siren go off outside. The ividcam turned on. "Good evening, citizens." Torrent's face beamed up through the hologram.

I put the cans that were in my hands down and ran over to the fire escape. Nana was already standing there with Lou.

"It is with a solemn heart that I address the nation today. A cowardly and evil act of war has taken out much of the United States population."

I looked down and saw Kai walking down the street. I put one leg out of the window and then the other. Nan and Lou didn't look away from the ividcam. I headed down the fire escape while the hologram of Torrent's large head continued talking above me.

"Twelve days ago, the United States was the target of an annihilation attempt by the New Russian Regime.

The Russian military released a bomb containing an unknown chemical into our atmosphere via their space station. This chemical has been tested at our highly advanced laboratories in a discrete location, and it has been determined by our top scientists that there is no antidote for its effects.

"Those affected by the gas are essentially asleep except for their muscle memory. The Sleeping will remain asleep forever. Therefore, we will be conducting the humane euthanasia of all those affected by the gas," Torrent's image spoke in the sky.

I reached the bottom of the fire escape and leaped down. I landed on my feet.

"Eleven days ago, we launched a nuclear weapon at Moscow, decimating their country and almost all of its inhabitants. Those who are left behind are few and helpless in an alien nation that was once Russia. We have also taken over their space station. Now we have complete control of outer space and all the satellites in circulation."

I stopped and looked up at the sky. *Destroyed Russia completely?* I let that sink in for a moment and then forced myself to continue moving.

Torrent's voice continued, "We have won this war, and we will rebuild this nation together. We will rebuild this *world* together. We must remain faithful and hopeful." She bowed her head as though to say a prayer.

I reached Kai. "Hey, how's your grandfather?" I asked.

Kai was looking up at the hologram. "He's okay. He's sleeping," Kai responded. "Not *that* kind of sleeping. Just sleeping," he clarified.

I guessed that that was something we would have to be very specific about now.

"They wanted to run a few tests. His protein levels were low."

I nodded. I looked at the apartment buildings around us. Heads poked out of some, but it was silent in the city other than the talking head in the sky.

"So, Russia, huh?" I asked, staring up at Torrent's hologram.

"Yeah, I guess so. Sons of bitches," he responded.

"Wow." I shook my head. "It just doesn't feel like it's over."

"That's cause it's not," Kai replied, still looking up.

I looked around our block. Our Division had 525 survivors. The national total of survivors was 55 million. That did not include the people plagued by side effects from the gas. They weren't considered survivors.

We started calling them Sleepers. The violent ones we called Night Terrors. The gas acted as a powerful sleeping agent that was intended to kill us upon inhalation, but for some people, the gas seemed to put their conscious minds to sleep and left their bodies awake with only the most primal senses intact. The different reactions among the Sleepers were thought to be caused by muscle memory and perhaps the subconscious of the individual. It was theorized that the violent Sleepers held angrier thoughts in their subconscious minds and all that rage was released by the gas. They had a thirst for violence and would attack anybody, tearing them limb from limb, with no recollection of whether they were once family or friend. The more subdued people were in life, the more they just waddled around and moaned as Sleepers. If that theory was true, then it should be no surprise that New York had a high rate of Night Terrors. We had the second highest rate of Night Terrors in the nation after Chicago.

The next two years were like living in a warzone. Soldiers, called the Forces, continued to clear out the dead and clean the streets. They were Torrent's men, and they patrolled night and day looking for Sleepers. The dead were incinerated in mass chambers, and the ash was buried in deep pits along the city's edges. Some of the Sleepers lingered in abandoned houses for months before either being caught or dying of natural causes. They did starve and freeze, but it took them awhile. Their bodies seemed more resilient and less affected by injury.

I saw one Sleeper shot square in the chest by the Forces, and still, he came charging at the soldier even with a gaping hole in his chest. The government said the gas's effects were irreversible, and they ordered the Sleepers to be killed on sight.

Curfew was put into effect so that the Forces could identify Sleepers out in the streets. For some reason, the Night Terrors seemed to become more agitated in the dark, and you could hear them screeching from all corners of the city when the sun went down. This wasn't to say they didn't come out during the day.

They did.

Sometimes you could mistake them for a homeless person or drug addict in the alley. It was difficult to tell the difference between the two, especially since the poverty and crime rate both spiked after the attack, leaving us in a world of rubble and rags. Most of us, at least.

The Elites remained sheltered behind their walls, while the dead were walking, and the living were dying.

Chapter Five

There was a line outside of the hospital about one hundred people deep. The director of the hospital, Orthel Delancey, was in front of the building speaking to the crowd. His glazed eyes and expressionless face mirrored his monotone voice as he spoke into the microphone.

"We are a free and complete healthcare service for the people," he spoke slowly and clearly. "We care about your needs, and we are here to help you. Please be patient as we are busy caring for other patients right now. Form a line, and you will be seen in the order in which you came."

A moment later he repeated the exact statement again. I walked through the crowd and listened to the director's robotic speech. It was as though he was set on repeat. The amount of injured and sick people was overwhelming. The crowd filled up half the parking lot in front of the building. My gaze moved from one person to the next, trying to analyze the situation. My eyes locked on a young girl. She was small, and she was held in her father's arms. Her eyelids flickered, revealing the whites of her eyes and then closed. Her father was yelling for help. I ran up to them and put a hand on the girl's head.

"How long has she been this way?" I asked.

"An hour maybe," he replied.

"Has she ever had a seizure before?"

"Yes, she has epilepsy."

"Does she not have medication?"

"We couldn't afford it this month." The girl's father spoke with tears in his eyes.

This child was in a *Status Epilepticus,* which meant she was in danger of permanent brain damage or death. I looked up toward Director Delancey who was in the process of repeating his statement again. "Please form a line, and you will be seen in the order in which you came."

"This girl needs to be seen now!" I yelled. The director continued to repeat his speech.

"Doctor, she needs to be seen now!" I demanded.

When Delancey began his speech from the beginning for the zillionth time, I knew I had no choice but to act.

I looked at the girl's father. "Take her inside and ask for Lee. Tell him El sent you."

The father didn't hesitate. He ran quickly through the crowd and into the building. Others began to object and tried to get into the building. I scanned the crowd and directed a gunshot victim to go inside as well.

"I need everyone with urgent and life-threatening injuries to move to the line inside and everyone else I need you to take a step back!" I demanded.

Some people began swarming toward the doors. I looked to see who was trying to come through. When a man with a bandage on his hand tried to move inside, I looked under the gauze. His finger was cut off at the tip.

"Put pressure on that. I know it hurts but right now it's not life-threatening. I promise you'll get seen today."

I looked at a woman who was pregnant and felt her head. She had a fever. I directed her inside. I glanced up at Director Orthel expecting him to be furious that I was taking charge, but he seemed unfazed by what was happening. I continued to sort the patients, locating a man with a gunshot wound to the abdomen. It looked like he was bleeding out, so I directed him inside. I saw another man limping. His ankle appeared to be fractured with bone protruding out of the skin.

"It's okay. I'm okay. I can wait. Take the people who need it more," urged the man.

I nodded.

I sent in a boy who couldn't breathe and an elderly man who appeared to be having a heart attack. Two of the men in line for lesser injuries lifted the man onto a gurney to help take him inside the building. I looked over the crowd once more. There was half the amount of people left outside. They were all in need of medical care, but I hoped they could hold on for a little longer.

"You will all be seen today," I promised before turning and running inside to help the urgent victims. I spent twenty-two hours in the hospital that day. The little girl who was having a seizure earlier had been treated with anti-seizure medicine. I walked over to her makeshift bed, which was a blanket on the floor. Her name was Lilly. She was eight-years-old and weighed thirty pounds. I looked at the father.

"She is skinny. Has she been eating?" I asked.

The girl looked down at the floor. I put my hand on her shoulder.

"I know the rationed food doesn't always taste the best, but we have to eat," I said, heading to the cupboard, and opening a small can of applesauce for her. She devoured it instantly. I stared at her in surprise.

"Doesn't look like the taste is the problem," I said, glancing at her father for an answer.

He looked away. He stood with his back toward me a minute longer. I walked over to the cabinet and grabbed a fruit cup for Lilly.

"Come to my home," the father finally said.

"Excuse me?" My eyes narrowed as I tried to understand the man's intent.

"I will show you why Lilly is this way," he said.

I didn't agree at first. I thought about it for a while and still hadn't had my mind made up by the time he had left. He told me his address, which was on the other end of the Division. When I finally left the hospital that day, I was physically and mentally exhausted. Every fiber in my being was telling me to get home and sleep. But the nurse in me wouldn't allow it. I wouldn't have been able to rest thinking about Lilly, anyway. If something was affecting her health at home, then maybe I could help.

So, I headed on foot across town. It was a twenty-five-minute walk. The sun had just begun to set and as it did the temperature dropped. It had begun to get colder and colder each day. I scanned the street for the address the man had given me; 55 Dolly Way.

A small white house sat pushed back along a narrow walkway with the number 55 painted above the front door. It was an old house with worn white shingles and a brick chimney. I imagined that the brown shutters once hung proudly in place by the sides of each window. Now there seemed to be more than a few shutters missing, and the ones that remained appeared to be hanging on by their last thread. The yard was covered with leaves, and trash littered the walkway to the front door. On the porch, more trash and old boxes appeared to be full of raggedy clothes. It was on the edge of the Division, so it was overlooking the water. The bright sun was setting behind me.

I knocked on the door once, and the father appeared. His eyes were solemn, and he looked at the ground as he opened the door.

"Come in." His words were muffled by a low hum I heard coming from the other room. I cautiously entered. The house was dim, but I could see there was a light coming from a bedroom in the back of the house.

"Where is Lilly?" I asked as I scanned the home. As my eyes adjusted, I could see my surroundings more clearly. There were photos of Lilly on the walls. She was at a much healthier weight in most of the pictures. We walked down the hall, and I peered into the first room we passed. The kitchen. There was an empty can of beans on the counter and something simmered in a pot on the stove.

"She is getting her mother ready for dinner," he responded.

He gestured for me to follow him and we walked deeper into the house toward the back bedroom. The windows appeared to be boarded behind the blinds, and a loud fan blew in the corner of the room. Lilly was placing a sheet around the neck of a woman in the bed. Then I noticed the ropes around the woman's ankles and wrists and then tied to the bedposts. She wriggled and moaned in a low tone.

"Oh my God," I gasped.

There was no doubt she was a Sleeper. Her face was scabbed with old blood, especially around her mouth. It appeared she had eaten some of her own lips. As I looked closer, I saw the infected sores on her body, probably from laying in her own excrement.

"I know what you're thinking," the father began.

I couldn't take my eyes off the woman. She gargled her tongue and bit at the air. I stared at her, and as I did, two thoughts ran wildly through my mind—*Help her! Kill her!*

In that order.

"Mommy is sick," Lilly whimpered. Those words spoken by her sweet eight-year-old voice broke my spell.

"Yes. She seems to be," I said. I cleared my throat. "Lilly, can you give your father and me a minute to talk?"

Lilly didn't move. She stood in place looking up at me as though she knew what I was thinking.

"Why don't you go wash up and set the table for dinner, Lilly," her dad added.

"Okay, Daddy," she said timidly and headed out of the room.

I heard her pitter patter down the hallway, and I waited until the sound was too far away to hear before I began. I reminded myself to watch my volume. If the Forces found out that the father had been hiding a Sleeper, both he and Lilly's mother would be euthanized. I didn't know what would happen to Lilly.

"What is this?" I demanded. "How could you let your daughter live like this?"

He remained calm and waited for me to take a breath.

"This is my wife. Her name is Martha Sanchez," he said matter-of-factly. "And she is my daughter's mother. How could I let them take her from us?"

"So, you chose to just let her rot here in front of your daughter?" I asked, looking once again at the woman's sores and scabs.

"I realize my actions may not have been the most rational. But I do not believe that my wife is dead. She is in there. I know it. I *feel* it."

His eyes filled with tears as he looked at his wife. I followed his gaze to the woman's hands tied up against the bed rail. I noticed the spot on her left hand where her ring used to be. It was slimmer and lighter than the rest of her skin, evidence of a finger that had worn a ring for many years.

My emotions had gotten the best of me. As I listened to his words, I understood his decision. His wife was still breathing and moving. I could imagine how difficult it must be to allow a loved one to be euthanized when you believed that person was still alive inside. Just because I understood where he was coming from didn't mean I would just brush aside science.

"There is no cure. The effects from the gas are permanent," I told him. "The euthanization doesn't hurt. It's quick. It's humane." I paused. There was more I was supposed to say, but I struggled to say it; what I had been taught to say by the hospital. "It's the law."

"It's murder," he responded. "I won't have my wife murdered."

"Is *this* living to you?" I pointed to his wife who was still chomping madly at the air and wriggling her legs in the ropes.

"You are a woman of medicine. How do you know there is no cure?" he asked.

I didn't have an answer for him. I thought for a moment before responding. "I don't know," I admitted.

"Exactly. You *don't* know."

Lilly appeared back in the room.

"Table is set for you and me, Daddy," she said with a smile. She was holding a small bowl of beans in her hands. She walked over toward her mother.

"Dinner time, Mommy," she said tenderly, as she sat in the chair next to her mother's bedside. Lilly began to spoon the beans into her mother's mouth.

"The government thinks she is dead," I said.

"Yes," he responded, as a matter-of-fact.

"You're splitting rations for two three ways," I surmised.

"Yes," he affirmed.

"And therefore, you have to choose between sedatives for your wife and seizure medication for Lilly." I was beginning to put the pieces together.

I watched Lilly as she fed her mother. She put one or two beans at a time on a spoon, and her mother chewed and swallowed. The woman didn't appear to be violent.

"Is she a Night Terror?" I asked, narrowing my eyes.

The sun had set, and the room was dim. If she were a Night Terror, I thought she would be more agitated by now. However, I also wasn't sure how many sedatives Mr. Sanchez had given her.

"No. She's not violent at all," he replied.

"Then why is she tied down?" I motioned toward the ropes on her ankles and wrists.

"As a precaution. She was wandering and falling before we tied her up. She was a danger to herself, not anyone else. She wouldn't hurt a fly." Mr. Sanchez looked down at his feet as he brought a hand to his face and wiped something from his eye.

I looked away. I could imagine what he was feeling, wanting to save someone so badly but not having the power. I felt that way when I lost my mother. I took a deep breath while I thought of our next move. I was relieved to hear that Lilly wasn't in danger with her mom in the house. But I also knew things couldn't stay this way for much longer. Even with the fan humming and the sedatives, someone would eventually hear her moans, and the Forces would find her. Plus, they couldn't keep splitting their meager rations. The multiple infections Lilly's mother was fighting were life-threatening. Something had to be done, but I could no longer argue that euthanizing her was the right decision. I couldn't argue it because I didn't believe it.

"Let me take her to the hospital so I can treat her infection," I finally said.

"No! Like you said the government thinks she is dead!" Mr. Sanchez exclaimed louder than I expected.

"I will enter her as a Jane Doe with mental illness," I assured him. When I noticed he wasn't convinced, I raised my voice slightly.

"She will die from the infections if they aren't treated."

It was the truth. She needed antibiotics, and topical solutions wouldn't suffice at this point. I needed to administer the medication through her bloodstream. It would be quicker and more effective that way. I had the resources I needed at the hospital plus we needed to get her out of that filthy bed. I had to figure out a way for the hospital to authorize an allowance for double medicine rations so that Lilly could get her seizure medication and Mrs. Sanchez could have her sedatives. I took a note in my head to send her home with a few sets of clean sheets, too.

He nodded his head, reluctantly. "I don't trust that hospital. But I trust you."

After just a few days of treating Mrs. Sanchez, her condition improved drastically. I kept a close eye on her throughout the day and was sure to give her a strong sedative at night to keep her subdued while I was off shift. By the weekend I thought it was best to send her home with antibiotics and mild sedatives that Mr. Sanchez could administer. I called him to come pick her up in the morning and told him that I would have her ready to go. The next morning, I arrived to work early to enter her discharge paperwork, but when I logged onto the computer and searched for her file, I couldn't find it.

I looked again.

Her file was still not showing up in the database. Hoping that it was a glitch in the computer system, I walked speedily to her room. The bed was empty. My heart fell to my stomach, and I spun around to find answers. The first person I saw was a janitor in the hallway.

"Where's my patient?" I asked urgently.

"I moved her," the janitor replied.

"Where did you move her?"

She just shrugged. Janitorial staff didn't have the authority to move a patient unless the patient was no longer a patient, but a body.

"Where did you move her?" I asked, louder and with more force.

Still, the woman just stared at me and shrugged. I jogged off swiftly heading to Director Orthel Delancey's office. I was trying to convince myself she was moved to another room or that maybe Mr. Sanchez picked her up late last night. I reached the fourth floor and headed to the far back office, which took up the entire north side of the building. I opened the door and walked in.

"Where is Patient 436?" I demanded. Director Delancey's office was immaculate. He had an orderly stack of papers in front of him, a bottle of water on a coaster to the right of his computer, and his ID Pass tucked to the side. He was barely startled by my abrupt entrance.

"436?" He sat blankly for a moment then his eyes lit up with sudden recollection. "Oh, yes. Euthanized last night." Then he slowly turned his face back down toward the papers in front of him.

I gasped and covered my mouth with my hand as though I was trying to catch the scream that I knew was coming out.

"No!" I felt a familiar helpless feeling taking over. I tried to keep my composure the best I could, but the lump in my throat was getting tighter. I moved my hand slightly away from my mouth to let the following words slip out. "Why?" The question leaked out of my mouth with a sob. "You didn't have to. She was someone's wife and someone's mother."

The Director's face was tilted down; he appeared to be reading one of the papers in front of him. It took him more than a few seconds to look up at me. When he did, he put down his pen and then stood up.

"There is no room or resources to treat or hold the Sleeping," he said, grabbing his work badge from the desk and putting it in his pocket. There seemed to be an extra ID badge dangling on Delancey's badge holder that caught my eye.

He knew she was a Sleeper. I couldn't help but feel responsible for bringing Mrs. Sanchez here. I couldn't remember now why I thought she would be safe at the hospital.

"Why then do we claim to be the free and complete health service station for all when really we mean free and complete for those we choose?" I raged. "She wasn't violent. She wasn't hurting anyone here!"

"Wasn't she?" Delancey didn't miss a beat. "She was taking up a bed ... a bed that someone else can now fill. You're the one who wanted shorter lines, Ms. Logan.

You can't have it both ways." He was so sure, and his lack of emotion set mine free.

"You don't get to choose who lives and who dies!" I yelled. My eyes kept moving to the ID badge in his hand. There *was* an additional badge there. It wasn't from the hospital. It looked like it had the Elite Village BK-Atlas logo on it. Delancey moved around to the side of his desk, and his progression toward me made me take a step back.

"What would you have us do? Take in all the Sleepers?" he asked.

I didn't have an answer. I just stood there trying to come up with something. But there was nothing I could say. After a moment the Director smiled. He took a step back and sat down, seemingly content with my response or lack thereof. He slid his two ID badges into the inside pocket of his white coat.

"Now, please close the door as you leave," he ordered, without looking up from the papers that were now back in front of him.

I turned around and closed the door behind me. I began walking slowly and tried to hold back my tears, but they filled my eyes nonetheless. As I opened the doors to my unit, I saw Lilly and her father standing right there in front of me with flowers. Mr. Sanchez didn't need to hear the words from my mouth because my face must have told it all. My eyes released a stream of tears as I opened my mouth to tell him what happened, but nothing came out. His eyes moved to the empty room where his wife used to be, and he lowered himself down into the waiting room chair.

I didn't move. I just stood there. "I am so sorry." The words came out shaken and hollow. They weren't enough.

He remained seated, looking down at the yellow and purple flowers he had brought for his wife. "She was gone long before she came here. You said it yourself. She was dead either way," he finally said.

Lilly climbed into her father's lap weeping uncontrollably. He took her into his arms. I noticed Lilly's weight gain immediately. She had filled out in just the one week her mother had been out of the house. Her wounds also looked healed, but what new emotional wounds this would bring no one could tell.

Chapter Six

It was five to nine in the evening, and the curfew was just about to begin. I lay down on the pullout couch wide-awake with Kai next to me. I replayed the conversation with Director Delancey in my head. I still didn't know the answer to his question, but it couldn't be murder. That couldn't be the answer. I was over at Kai's apartment a lot of the time now since his grandfather passed away several months earlier. Mr. Maxwell was never the same after the gas attack, and he died of natural causes not too long after. We cremated his body on the roof and spread his remains in the rose garden along with Mom and Mrs. Carter.

We heard the screeching of the Night Terrors begin outside.

"Close the blinds," I told Kai. It was best not to draw attention to yourself or your apartment. It only brought the Night Terrors or the Forces in closer. While the Night Terrors seemed to prefer hiding in the shadows during the day, they were attracted to bright lights and loud noises, so remaining quiet after curfew was wise. It was also wise because the Forces took curfew very seriously. We had heard on many occasions of curfew offenders being taken away and never seen or heard from again. Kai turned off the lights and lit a candle, placing it on the coffee table in front of us. We turned the living room into a fortress of sorts with weapons lining the kitchen counter, and boards, nails, and a hammer waiting in the hallway if needed.

We had pillows and blankets, and we stationed ourselves on the pullout couch. For some reason, it felt safer there than in either of the two bedrooms. We kept his grandfather's room locked up, and Kai's room was more for show because he fell asleep with me in the living room every night.

The screaming outside seemed louder than usual tonight. Kai lay down next to me, and we began our nightly ritual of unraveling our thoughts.

"The doctors at the hospital have been acting so strange lately," I began.

"How so?" Kai asked.

"I can't really put my finger on it. The way they talk and act ... it's just so robotic. I saw on Dr. Delancey's calendar that he has been going to the Charter School every night at seven. He has an ID Pass to Atlas, too."

Kai's eyes shifted to me when I mentioned the school.

"Maybe he's been lecturing there," he offered.

"No, I would know about that. It's something else. I just don't know what." I deliberated as I spoke.

"What are you thinking?"

"I don't know, but I'd love to get behind those walls to find out."

The Charter School was for the Elites' kids in the neighborhood BK-Atlas. It was a large stone building at the center of the Village of Atlas. The Village itself was encompassed by a fifteen-foot stone wall with checkpoints at every entrance. The only way to access the Village was with an ID Pass.

Kai turned his gaze back up to the ceiling. His breathing was quiet, but his thoughts were loud. I examined his face. His eyebrows were furrowed, and his jaw was tense.

I propped myself up on an elbow. "What is it?" I asked.

"Are you tired?" he responded, not looking away from the ceiling.

"No, not at all," I replied, staring wide-eyed at Kai.

He finally returned my gaze. "There's something I've wanted to tell you," he said.

"Kai ..." I began. I knew he had feelings for me, but I also knew that a relationship would ruin our friendship and it was something we had spoken about in the past.

"No, El. Not that," he chuckled. "I know I repulse you in every way. Something else."

"Repulse me?" I sat up fully. "The opposite!" I exclaimed with my eyebrows raised.

Kai looked straight into my eyes, and I felt my heart flutter.

Part of me hoped he would profess his undying love for me, kiss me, and take me far away from here. Part of me wanted to run away with him to the middle of nowhere where we could live out our lives completely and totally in bliss. I could never leave Lou or Theo, though. Dad and Nan would never leave the apartment so this fantasy of mine would remain just that. I snapped myself out of it. "What is it you want to tell me?" I asked.

Kai didn't say anything. He just stood up and grabbed me by the hand. We walked out of the living room and turned down the hall, stopping in front of his grandfather's bedroom door. I was staring at him and then at the door, confused but curious. He didn't let go of my hand. With his free hand, he reached up to the top of the doorframe where we had hidden the key five months ago. He hesitated for a moment and then unlocked the door.

It opened with a squeak.

I hadn't been in here since right after Kai's grandfather passed away. After we had taken his body to the roof and burned it, we came back down here and locked up this room. Kai let go of my hand and walked toward his grandfather's closet. Still not speaking, he opened the closet door, and I looked inside. There was old government issued garb and white lab gear with the Atlas badge sewn in on the lapel.

"Your grandfather was an Elite?" I gasped.

Kai didn't respond. He parted the clothing and pushed aside the garb to reveal a hidden shelf in the back of the closet.

I was still staring at the clothing. How could I not have known this? *Of course, Kai is an Elite. Look at him!* I scanned the rest of the closet. On the shelf was a book. I reached for it, half expecting Kai to stop me. But he didn't. I opened the book and began scanning the photos and notes inside. There were pictures of lab workers, animals in cages, and Rations Centers. It seemed liked scientists were conducting some kind of testing on the animals. I flipped through the pages and saw similar images of labs with different scientists and more animals. Then I stopped on a photo of Kai's grandfather.

The caption below the photo read: *Sr. Scientist M. Maxwell receiving the coveted Continuity Award.* The Continuity Award was the highest honor given to those who preserved the Elites' way of life. I turned the page to another photo of Kai's grandfather shaking hands with Torrent. My eyes steadied and narrowed. I didn't read the caption. I just stared at the image.

Kai finally broke his silence. "He developed an additive for food. He thought it would bring more nutrition in less quantity, filling people up quicker ... less food while maintaining caloric consumption. His team ran tests on animals, and they were successful in all the trials. He was a hero not just to the Elites, but to everyone. But then the animals started dying. They developed tumors, cancer, and neurological disorders. He continued to run tests and found that the food additive was toxic in the long term. It was causing developmental and neurological damage to the animals. He told the FDA what he had discovered, but the government didn't care. They continued to use the additive. It was saving them billions of dollars, and they didn't eat Ration food, anyway."

"It is still in the food we eat?" I asked.

Kai didn't respond. He just paused briefly then continued talking.

"My parents still work for the government. Or at least they did the last I heard. They're researchers. I grew up in the Elite Village. When my grandfather threatened to tell the people what the government was doing, he was kicked out of the facility and out of Atlas. They threatened to kill my mother if he told anyone about the research. So, Grandfather stayed quiet. He believed it was better to live and die with the people, than live among Elites.

"I'm not from Division Two like I had told you. I lived in the Elite Village before I moved here. I went to private schools. I ran away when I was eleven to live here with my grandfather. My parents never came looking for me, but I don't regret it." Kai said the words like they were a confession, and when he had finished, he held his breath for judgment. Truth is, it explained a lot about Kai.

"Why did you wait until now to tell me? No, *how* could you wait until now to tell me?" I demanded. I was angry about what the government was doing to our food, but I was furious at Kai for lying to me for so long.

"I always wanted to tell you. I just didn't know how you would react."

"You should have told me anyway!" I replied louder than I had intended. We heard a screech from outside, and we both looked toward the window. We paused for a moment. Then Kai continued more quietly.

"I know. And I'm sorry." I saw the sincerity in his eyes. Staying mad at Kai was difficult.

"You went to the school?" I asked.

"Yes."

"Well, what was it like there?" I asked with genuine curiosity. I saw the tension in Kai's eyes ease probably because he realized that I wasn't going to hold a grudge against him for his lies.

He smiled. "Terrible. Just how you would picture it. The teachers force down your throat the idea that the government is good, and that the people should be compliant. They indoctrinate everyone to act and sound just like them. Individual thoughts aren't acceptable. They have strict rules on what topics can be discussed and then have broad conversations within those few topics to make it seem like free thought is encouraged. But it is all a sham."

"Do you know Torrent?" I asked.

"No, I never met her personally. She came to the school occasionally to meet with the board and chairmen, but she never stopped and talked to the students."

"Did you date anyone there?" I asked in more of a whisper because I was ashamed of the fact that the thought had even crossed my mind.

Kai couldn't hide his smile although he tried because he could see I was serious.

"No, no one."

Good. Now that we got that out of the way I could obtain some answers about what was going on behind those walls. Even though it was eight years ago, there must be some clues.

"Well, what else do they teach there?" I asked.

"Our lesson plans were like yours. We were taught that Torrent and her administration were the Founding Fathers in a new era of the United States, rewriting the Constitution, all for the best of course." Kai's voice was full of sarcasm. Torrent's administration rewrote the Constitution to be by the government, for the government—that much was clear.

Even before the war, there was so much suffering. It didn't make sense to us that we were taught to praise a president for healing a country that was in smithereens.

"Where did the board have their meetings?" I asked.

"In the school. The far-left wing of the fourth floor is where the chairman of Atlas had his office. The meetings were conducted in an office just outside of that wing." Kai looked up as he thought about the layout of the school.

"There were more offices down the hall, and the classrooms were on the second and third floors. Then there was a café one floor down with a candy shop, too."

"You must miss that," I said, thinking about how different his life must have been back then.

"Leaving that Village is the best thing that ever happened to me."

My eyes shifted to Kai quickly.

"Other than meeting you, of course," he added with a smile.

I smiled back.

Kai sighed. "My grandfather never wanted to cause any harm. He always taught me that science helped people and that one scientist could change the world. He just didn't take into consideration that change can move in two directions." Kai lowered his eyes.

I put my hand on his arm. "It's not his fault. It's Torrent's. He tried to tell her, and she didn't listen," I reassured him.

"The night he left, my parents sat me down and told me we weren't to speak of him again. His name was forbidden in our home. They took down all the photos of him that we had hanging on the walls. It was like he never existed. After that, I was alone most of the time.

"My parents worked all the time, so it was Grandfather who had played baseball with me, helped me with my homework, and taught me how to ride a bike. My friends and I would go to the arcade, swim at the lake, and ride bikes in the woods, but they always went home to their families afterward. I went home to an empty house. I left to find him because I knew I was better off out here with him than in there without him.

I thought maybe we could help bring an end to all the suffering. But once we were out here, we were silenced. Not only did we lack the resources; we didn't have voices. We couldn't tell anyone what was happening inside the walls."

"Where are your parents now?" I asked.

"I don't know. Still there, maybe. Or dead," he responded as though he didn't care one way or another, but he failed at covering up the sadness in his voice.

I looked back toward the closet. I understood why Kai was angry with them. It wasn't easy to forgive someone when you felt like they had abandoned you.

"So now you know what happens behind the wall," he continued.

He looked at his grandfather's book and then at me. His features hardened, and his body tensed. It was impossible to tell if he was thinking about Torrent, his grandfather, his parents, or all three. But something weighed heavily on his mind.

"What it is?" I asked.

"Maybe it isn't about the politics. Maybe that never even mattered." He paused and then took a step closer. "We can move somewhere far away from all this. It could be just you and me."

His voice was still angry, but angelic in perfect harmony. All the rage in his body gave way to something much more soothing but equally intense. He put his arm around my waist and pulled me in close. My stomach turned into a knot. He lifted his other hand to my face and brushed a strand of hair off of my cheek, tucking it behind my ear.

"You don't look repulsed," he breathed. He took another step closer into me, which pushed me up against the frame of the closet door just in time before my knees gave out. He guided me down slowly as we sank to the floor.

"Kai," I whispered.

"I love you," he said.

I closed my eyes and felt the heat from his mouth on mine. But before I had time to surrender to his words, we heard a scream.

I instinctively turned my gaze to the window.

"That doesn't sound like a Night Terror," I said with what little air I could push from my lungs.

We heard it again, and it brought us to our feet.

Kai instinctively blew out the candle, and at the same time, we headed toward the window.

"Get down," he ordered. Kai kneeled to the floor, and I did the same next to him. He drew back the curtains carefully. The night looked still outside. The sun had fully set, but the city street was illuminated by the streetlights below. I heard some distant Night Terrors, but nothing more. We waited in silence, hearing only the steady sound of our breathing. Then out of the corner of my eye, I saw movement.

"There," I said, pointing. A small figure darted from behind a car and headed down toward the park.

"I think it's a kid," I said.

"He could be a Sleeper." Kai said it, but we both were thinking it.

The small figure stayed still behind a large tree. Then a little head peeked out from the darkness, glancing back toward the street and quickly retreating into the shadows. He was hiding from something.

"We have to go help him," I said. "If either the Night Terrors or the Forces find him, he's dead."

"Or he could be a Night Terror," Kai insisted.

Kai was right, but I had never seen a Night Terror hide like that before. I was going to find out either way, and I knew Kai wouldn't let me go by myself.

"Come on," I said.

The fire escape was off of the living room. I headed straight for the window while Kai headed toward the kitchen counter and grabbed the biggest knife we had. I quickly unlocked the window and lifted the pane, and then the screen. Kai came over and poked his head out of the window from behind me.

"I'll go first." He pushed ahead of me and with one swift move he had both of his legs out of the window before I could object. He was already climbing down the ladder while I climbed out much more awkwardly, one leg at a time behind him. We descended the stairs in complete silence, other than the occasional creak from the old steel. Kai took his final leap from the first-floor landing to the ground like a cat. I knew my jump wouldn't be so graceful. He waited below for me, and as I approached the landing, he reached out his arms.

I let myself fall into them. We were in the shadows, but the street was lit up with the neon city lights. If we were going to get across it, we had to do it quickly and quietly. We stayed low and moved like bandits in the nights. Kai approached the road first and looked around.

"Let's go," he whispered, as he darted across the road, staying low to the ground.

He looked back once to make sure I was low, as well. We reached the park and took cover in the shadows once again.

I saw the kid curled in a ball under the same tree he had been hiding behind when we saw him from the apartment. He was bloodied. But it didn't appear to be *his* blood.

We walked closer to him cautiously.

"Hey, buddy, Kai said softly, trying to get a look at the kid's face.

The kid didn't look up or speak. I glanced around to make sure no one else was nearby.

Kai tried talking to the child again.

"Hey, you're going to be okay. We are here to help you."

The boy looked up. His dirty face was streaked with tears.

"My mom and dad!" The kid cried loudly.

"Shh ..." Kai said quickly, putting a hand over the kid's mouth. "We have to keep our voices small, okay? What's your name?"

"Billy." The kid held back his tears.

"Hi, Billy. I'm Kai, and this is El," Kai whispered. "Come on. We are going to get you out of here." Kai reached down for the kid and scooped him up effortlessly, but he squealed.

"No! I want my mom and dad!" he sobbed.

"Shut up! Okay! Okay!" Kai exclaimed as he lowered the kid. "You want to get us all killed? Where is your mom?"

"They took her in their truck," the boy sobbed quietly.

"The Forces took her?" I asked.

The boy nodded his head. I could tell Kai was thinking about how to phrase his next question appropriately for a child.

"Were your parents acting ... differently?" Kai asked the question, and we both watched Billy for his response.

The boy shook his head. Then he stood up and peeked his head around the tree that we were hiding behind. Kai went to stop him, but Billy turned right back around to us.

"In that truck over there," he said, pointing up the street. I extended my neck around the tree and saw a black truck pulled to the side of the street about a block and a half away. From the blacked-out windows to the long antenna on top it was easy to tell that it was a government vehicle.

"I didn't see that truck there before," Kai said, looking down at Billy. "That means they're driving around. Probably looking for you. I'll go see if I can find your mom if you go upstairs with my friend, El."

"What? No!" I cried. "*You* go up with him. I'll go see if she is in the truck."

"That's not happening. We don't even know if Forces are waiting in that truck," Kai said firmly.

"Forces could be in this park right now. We are wasting time arguing about it."

Not only were we breaking curfew, but we were also possibly aiding and abetting the kid in escaping from the Forces, the penalty for which would surely be death.

"We have a better chance of being seen with him. Take him upstairs," Kai ordered.

Billy looked back and forth between the two of us each time we spoke.

"I am smaller so I can more easily hide in the shadows, but you are stronger, so you can carry Billy," I argued. "I wouldn't even be able to get up onto the fire escape without you." It made sense to me, but I might as well have been trying to convince Kai that the sky was green based on the way he was staring at me.

"We are wasting time," I added, annoyed.

"Let's just all go together," Billy finally offered.

We both glanced down at him.

"Fine, but *you* have to stay quiet," Kai sighed. The boy nodded.

I poked my head out of the shadows and around the tree. The street sounded quiet and looked just as still.

"Let's go," I said.

The three of us cautiously began running up the block toward the truck—Kai in front, followed by the small boy holding my hand. There were no signs of the Forces. They must have been in the nearby parks and alleys looking for Billy. We approached the truck and kneeled behind it. After catching his breath for a moment, Kai stood up slowly and peeked his head into the back window, and then he crouched back down, and we gathered into a huddle.

"There is a woman inside," he whispered. "Now either the doors are locked or they only open from the inside. Either way, the second we get the door opened we need to run." Billy and I both nodded.

Just then I saw movement out of the corner of my eye. I looked up the street a little further and saw something on the sidewalk. It took my mind a moment to decipher what I was seeing.

It was a body.

A man's, and it was face down. A cane lay on the ground less than a foot away from the body. Judging by the amount of blood surrounding the man, I assumed he was dead. The movement I had seen was a rat that had come to eat the fresh flesh.

"Oh my God," I shuddered as I turned the boy's face away. I used my body to block his view. I motioned to Kai with my eyes, and he looked over his shoulder to see what I had seen. He took a deep breath looking around. The Forces couldn't be far. They wouldn't have left a body lying on the ground for long.

"Okay," he said. "We need to move quickly." Kai stood up and peered back into the truck. "Hello?" he whispered.

I heard a weak voice from the back of the truck.

"Please, please," she begged.

Her words were clear, not like the slurs and gargles of a Sleeper.

"I'm going to try to open the door," Kai said, jiggling the handle. It was locked.

"I need you to unlock the doors," he told the woman. She was mumbling something, but I couldn't make it out.

"Can you do that? Can you unlock the doors?" Kai repeated. "There should be two buttons by the handle. I need you to push the one on the right." There was a long pause.

I started to squirm, thinking about how close the Forces would be by now. This might have been a bad idea. Bad enough to get us killed.

"We have a boy here," Kai said. "Billy."

There was another long pause, and then we heard the doors unlock. Kai opened the door quietly. No alarm sounded. He picked up the woman almost effortlessly.

"Come on," he said, looking over his shoulder at me. We crept quickly down the street; the boy close to my side.

"My son?" the woman asked faintly.

"He is right here," I said.

"Mommy," the boy whispered.

The woman released a sigh of relief and passed out in Kai's arms. We heard rustling in the park behind us, and then voices. The Forces were moving in closer. They were going to notice that the woman was missing any minute.

It was too dangerous to take them up the fire escape, so we headed to the front entrance of the building and hurried down into the basement. That place still gave me nightmares. We had cleaned the shelter out well. Dad had placed a table down there with chairs, and we set up a few cots. We had water and medical supplies stocked against the far-left wall.

Kai laid the woman down on one of the cots and covered her with a wool blanket from the supply rack. She was bleeding badly. I looked at her wounds. The one that worried me the most was the deep gash on her forehead. It was possible that she could have had a concussion as well. "She lost a lot of blood. She'd benefit from an IV," I said. "I can get one from the hospital."

"You can get one tomorrow," Kai said. "It's after eleven. Curfew isn't over until six. That's seven hours. We can wait."

I knew he was right. Going out now would be too risky with the Forces right outside. We gave the woman antibiotics and cleaned her wounds. She would be able to make it until the morning.

Kai was sleeping sitting up in a chair at the table, and I had just fallen asleep on a cot nearby when the woman woke up with a jerk four hours later. We found out that she worked as a TV reporter out of Chicago. Her name was Gianna Grace. She had come to New York with her husband and their son to work on a story involving unethical human experimentation. She said that a source had tipped her off that Atlas was at the center of the operation and that Mr. Berea, chairman of the Charter School, oversaw the classified work.

"Is it a government operation?" I asked.

"We don't know," Gianna said. "All we know is that many reporters and politicians have been going missing, and then they turn up ... altered."

Altered. I let that word bounce around my head for a moment.

"Like Delancey with his robotic speeches," I said, glancing over at Kai. His mouth was in a straight tight line. I knew I wasn't going to get a response from him. I turned back over to Gianna.

"Who is your source?" I asked.

"I can't give up a source," Gianna responded. "Besides, I don't even know their name. We corresponded via portal and only through typed encrypted Latin. Our conversations were kept short and sweet." Portals had the capability of projecting scanned images of the user's face and body into the room of other portals for virtual meetings; however, this feature would have been avoided if one were trying to remain anonymous.

"And they told you these experiments were being conducted in Atlas by the chairman of the Charter School?" I clarified.

"They said that they had reason to believe the Charter School was the headquarters for the experiments under the direct supervision of Berea himself," she said, taking a sip of water.

"And you think you can trust this ... source?" I asked as I sat down on the cot right next to hers.

"They're not without merit. The same source led a colleague of mine to the body of Hansel Lorne, the astronaut who claimed he had watched the gas attack and the ensuing war from outer space. He was murdered in what many thought was a government cover-up. Plus, this source knew details about the inside of the Elite Village that only someone with special security clearance could know."

"We aren't the first to begin considering stories like these. Other reporters, colleagues of mine, began documenting reports of suspicious government activity before the Russian strike. Some say that Torrent knew about the strike days in advance. Some say that she has an antidote to the sleeping agent, but she won't release it to the public. But these are all just conspiracy theories unless they are proven to be true. Our team was once the largest news network in the United States. Now we are made up of barely thirty reporters across the entire fifty states, and of those reporters, I can tell you, many aren't the same anymore. I think you know that even considering any story like the ones I've just mentioned is punishable by death," Gianna said.

I sat still and continued to listen to her speak.

"Johan Berea's office is in the Atlas school within the Elite Village. Billy's father, Himey, was posing as an Elite from Chicago's Elite Division, Albatross."

"Did he use a cane?" I asked.

"Yes," she said, surprised by the question.

I looked over at Kai and back to Gianna. My face must have said it all. Her gaze trailed off.

"I'm so sorry," I said, placing my hand on her shoulder.

"Himey and I weren't a couple. We met as young reporters over a decade ago while both working on a story. We haven't been together since shortly after Billy was born. Truth be told, we were barely friends anymore, but we had been working on this story ..." Her words trailed off.

I moved my hand to her forehead to feel for a fever. She was still warm and probably dehydrated. I stood up and poured her another cup of water. She would benefit from an IV and rest. I knew more than ever that I had to get behind those walls.

Chapter Seven

At six that morning, I headed to the hospital to get the medical supplies, leaving Kai behind to watch over Gianna and Billy with strict orders for Gianna to rest. Lee was already at work behind the front desk at our station. He saw me immediately as I entered the floor.

"Hi, El," he called to me.

"Oh, hey." I failed in my attempt to respond casually. I always looked stiff when I was hiding something. It seemed like if I moved too much, the truth would find its way out of me. I didn't want to stop for small talk, and more importantly, I didn't want him to ask me any questions. I worried he saw through my façade.

"What are you doing here? You're not on the schedule today," he asked.

I should have known that he would know my work schedule. "I know. I'm just here for some supplies," I said, as I headed over to the supply closet. I heard him push his chair back and I knew he had begun following me.

"What for?" he asked, now right behind me.

"Wounds, dehydration, and blood loss," I answered.

Lee paused for a moment, staring at me and then at the supplies. "You're going to need an IV and saline," he said, as he pushed in front of me to grab an empty box. He began putting items in it. "Saline, extra saline," he said to himself as he loaded up the box.

I watched him.

"Are you going to need sutures?" he asked.

I shook my head. "Maybe just some antibiotic," I said.

When he was done filling up the box he turned and looked at me. "There," he announced proudly.

I went to take the box from him, but he turned his body away.

"No, it's heavy. I'll carry it for you."

Lee was about the same size as me and was probably just as physically strong.

"No, it's fine, Lee. You have to stay here and watch the unit," I said, as I went to grab the box again. He turned his body the other way.

"No, I'm off. I worked the overnight."

I glanced at the front desk and saw Shelly, another nurse, taking her jacket off and placing it on the back of the chair. I turned back to Lee who was smiling. I rolled my eyes.

"Okay," I said reluctantly.

On the walk back to the apartment I told him what happened. Well, some of it. It wasn't that I didn't trust Lee, I just didn't want him to become involved with something that could get him hurt or killed. Plus, if one of the doctors started asking him questions, it would probably be best if he didn't have to lie. I'd seen him lie before and he was even worse at it than me.

We walked into the apartment and down the stairs to the shelter. Kai was sitting on the cot playing cards with Billy while Gianna watched. The three of them looked up at us.

"Hi. This is Lee," I said, gesturing to Lee.

"Hi Lee," Billy said, waving. Gianna just smiled.

Lee said he would administer the IV and clean Gianna's wounds.

I wanted to try sneaking into the Village. I had a plan to take Kai's old school ID Pass and check out the chairman's office to see if I could find any proof to back up Gianna's story. But I didn't want Kai to follow me. I knew I had to make something up.

"Anyone want some coffee?" I asked. "I was going to head down to the Rations Center and grab some."

"Yes please!" Gianna responded eagerly.

"I'll come with you," Kai began.

"No. You stay and watch over everything here." I lowered my voice and added, "Make sure they don't try to leave until we know what's going on." I said this to ensure he would stay behind. We were fugitives now, after all.

Kai nodded.

I headed upstairs to Kai's apartment and then over to Mr. Maxwell's closet. I grabbed the box off the shelf and rummaged through it until I found Kai's ID Pass. There was a huge "KM" on the front. Kai Maxwell. I ran out of the apartment swiftly closing the doors behind me. My foot had just hit the first step when I heard a door open nearby.

"Kai?" It was my father's voice.

I thought about making a run for it or hiding somewhere, but I knew he would catch me either way.

"Hi, Dad," I called out.

"El!" he exclaimed happily. Since we were neighbors, it was strange that I hadn't seen him in over a week.

"Where are you going?" he asked, as he walked further out into the hallway.

"To the hospital," I lied. "I'm going to cover Lee's shift. He has to attend a thing with his uncle." It scared me how easy it was to lie. I knew if he even suspected in the slightest that I was up to anything dangerous, he would die trying to stop me. I didn't want him to become involved.

"How have you been?" he asked, walking toward me.

"I'm great, Dad," I said. "I've been taking on extra shifts. We've been so busy with everything." I hoped he would let me continue on my way once he heard just how busy I had been.

"You are overworked," Dad said. "Don't take on more than you can bear. You are too much like me in that way. Your patients may need you, but you need to take care of yourself, first."

"I'm fine, really. I love my job. It keeps me busy."

Dad waited and analyzed my face for a moment. *Can he tell I'm making this all up as I go along?* I waited for his response.

"Where is Kai?" he asked finally.

"Oh, I think he went fishing," I lied.

"Fishing, eh?" Dad asked with a smile. I knew Dad loved to fish. "Tell him to come get me next time. Has he snuck in any hunting? I caught a deer two weeks ago ... I thought we had enough to last throughout the season, but between your grandma and your sister it looks like I'll have to make another trip." Dad chuckled. Hunting and fishing were illegal since there was no public land for citizens to use, but that didn't stop many people from searching for their own food since rations were so scant.

"Yeah," I laughed. "Lou came by the other day before she went down to her bus. She told me about that. I'm sorry I don't come by more often, it's just with work and everything—"

"No need to apologize, El. You are twenty-one-years-old ... a woman now. I understand that." Dad's voice cracked slightly when he spoke. His tan skin wrinkled around his eyes and mouth. I knew he missed me. I knew he missed Mom, too. Guilt began to build in the pit of my stomach.

"Your grandmother barely gets out of bed anymore, so I'm here with her a lot of the time. Otherwise, I would be visiting you," he said with an apologetic smile.

"Let's eat dinner together next week," I said. "Like old times. Me, you, Nan, Lou and I'll even try to find Theo around."

"That sounds good, Elisha. And invite Kai, too. Tell him I like trout and blackfish."

I had already forgotten that I had lied about Kai fishing. I guessed we might have to really go catch some fish.

"If they're biting, that is," I responded warily.

"Oh, they're biting. An old friend of mine down at the Rec Center said he caught over a dozen trout last week."

"Oh," I said. "Good. That's good." It wasn't good. I knew nothing about fishing, and I was sure that Kai had never touched a worm before. We would be the blind leading the blind.

"Why wait until next week?" Dad offered. "I can come by tonight and help Kai clean his catches."

I put my hand in my pocket to feel the ID Pass inside. I was on a mission. No more distractions. One of the main reasons that I needed to find out what was going on behind the walls of BK-Atlas was because I cared about my family.

I took a deep breath. "Tonight's not going to work. We have plans." I left it at that. I was hoping he would, too.

"I see." His brown eyes looked to the floor and then back at me. "Okay." He shrugged and tried his best to smile. "Next week is good, too."

I grinned. "I have to go. I don't want to be late." I stood there for a moment trying not to seem too eager to leave. I had to stop my leg from bouncing.

"Okay, we will see you next week then," he said as he closed the distance between us, kissing my cheek.

"Okay!" I said, and I turned to dodge down the stairs. "Bye!" I called out as I darted down the steps quickly.

I had missed my family. Since my mom died, it was difficult to be around them. I knew that he felt it too. Mom was the glue of our family and when she died it all kind of fell apart. Dad took care of Nan who was only getting older, and Lou spent a lot of time at the Rec Center by the school. I think being home without our mother was hard for her, too. It had been over a year since she had passed away. Theo was out and about with the BK12, I assumed.

I headed to Atlas. I knew it was a long shot to think that Kai's ID Pass would still work after all these years. Who was to say that the card wasn't deactivated when Kai left the Village for the city? My plan was really a non-plan. I was going to try to scan the card, and if it worked, I was going to enter Atlas, find Mr. Berea's office, and look for ... something. If the card didn't work, I was going to run.

I neared the walls of the Village. The stone wall was over fifteen-feet tall. There were only four ways in and out of the Village, and that was through the exit and entry ports on each of the four sides of the giant wall that was Atlas. Each port had a security officer attending it. The officer sat in a bulletproof glass booth perched on top of the wall.

As I walked up to the port, I noticed it was more advanced than our turnstiles at the Rations Center. I had never been this close to notice before. There wasn't a turnstile at the port at all, actually. There was a large metal panel as thick as the wall itself that seemed to be built upon a sliding mechanism.

I looked up and saw the security officer peer down from his booth. I took Kai's ID Pass out of my pocket and placed it on the scanner. There was a loud beep and a pause, and then the metal door slid open allowing me to walk through. I glanced from the corner of my eye to see if the security officer was watching.

He wasn't.

I took a deep breath and walked inside. The doors closed behind me. Then I heard the microphone screech from the security booth. I spun around quickly.

"Kai Maxwell. Get your ID Pass photo fixed!" he shouted down to me. I stood frozen in terror.

"Get your ID Pass fixed at the tech center," the security officer repeated into the microphone. "Your photo won't load."

I nodded and turned back around quickly. We didn't have photos attached to our ID Passes in the Divisions. It figured that the Elites' security would be a little tighter. I figured Kai's photo was removed after he fled Atlas. Whether his ID Pass working was an oversight or intentional was a mystery to me. But I was in and for now, I was safe.

Atlas was even more beautiful than I had imagined. Kai had explained to me that the Village was set up into four districts: the Shopping District, the Residential District, the Business District, and the School District. A large pond sat in the center of the area I had entered, which appeared to be the Shopping District. A fountain that sprayed water majestically adorned the pond. Music played from speakers built into the light posts that stood around the walkway that encircled the water. To the left were the houses—the Residential District I assumed. There were roughly two hundred homes, and they were large, each with a front porch and a fenced in backyard.

People were walking around on the sidewalks and moving in and out of shops. Children ran with ice cream cones, and a group of teenagers read comic books under a tree at the park. I heard a horn honk.

"Move onto the sidewalk, young lady," a man in a red 2030 Corvette hollered with a wave of his hand and a smile.

I looked around. I hadn't realized I was standing right in the middle of the intersection. Oncoming traffic was heading my way from both directions.

"Oh!" I exclaimed as I hurried up onto the sidewalk. "Thanks." I waved back at the man.

He didn't seem to notice that I was an outsider in spite of my appearance. My torn jeans must have been handed down numerous times before landing in my possession, and my T-shirt was one of my father's from the 2020s. I guess my outfit could be considered trendy. *I'll never understand these people.*

I watched the people driving by for any indications of suspicion, but I didn't see any. Maybe I would be able to find what I was looking for after all. I started walking deeper into the Village. I wasn't exactly sure where the school was, but I thought I would be able to recognize it if I saw it. I headed right toward the tall buildings in the distance—the Business District.

Before I reached the buildings, I saw a street sign at an intersection. It was perched on a pole and simply read *School.* There was an arrow pointing to the left below the sign. I turned down that street and continued walking for what felt like forever. That's when I started seeing kids my age, and a little younger—high-schoolers. A large red brick building came into view. It was massive. It stretched five city blocks in width and what looked to be five in length, as well.

I made my way up the broad cement stairs toward the front doors. I hadn't reached the top when a group of Elite girls came hopping out of the building. They paused to stare at me and then whispered to each other as they sneered and walked away. I squirmed. Once again, I felt like an outsider. I looked around to see if anyone else was watching me. There didn't appear to be anyone looking, but I knew I had to make this quick, regardless.

I sped to the top of the steps and opened the large doors. The grand corridor was a dark shade of red with gold light fixtures and mirrored chandeliers. Gilt-framed portraits of what I assumed were former teachers and staff hung on the walls. The hustle and bustle from both children and teachers alike swept me through the entrance and into its flow. There was a hallway branching off of each side of me, and a staircase straight ahead. I remember Kai saying that Mr. Berea's office was on the fourth floor. I darted quickly to the stairs and headed up. I rounded the corner to the fourth floor, but I didn't make it halfway up before a woman stopped me in my tracks.

"Oh!" I cried, alarmed by her presence.

"And what are you doing here?"

"I ..." I was thinking of running.

"You should be in class!"

"Oh, yes," I said, relieved that she had mistaken me for a student.

"Is there a reason you are heading to the Paragon?"

"The Paragon?"

"Yes, the top floor, Miss. Is that where you are going?" the woman asked condescendingly.

"Yes, I needed to go there," I replied.

"Oh, you are part of the student council!" the woman exclaimed as though she had had an epiphany. "Well hurry on, then. They've begun the lecture without you."

"Okay," I said, and I walked slowly around her.

"Well, hurry!" she said loudly.

I ran. Once the woman was no longer in sight, I stopped. *That was a close one, too close for my liking.* I looked around for any sign of the chairman's office. "Left-wing," I remembered Kai saying. I darted to the left, but other than a large red door, it was a dead end. There were two glass windows on each side of the door, allowing me to see in. Inside there was a long foyer with plants and light fixtures, and at the end of the foyer was dome-shaped room.

That must be Berea's wing. I didn't see anyone inside, so I tried the door handle. To my surprise, it was unlocked. I opened the door carefully and stepped inside. The hallway had white marble floors that made tiptoeing difficult. I opted for speed walking instead. The tables that aligned the long entryway were heavily decorated with glassware, fabrics, sculptures, and candles. I hurried to the end of the hallway, and into the large dome shaped room. There were numerous doors on any given side of the dome. If I was an Elite and I was to pick an office, I would want the one with the view. I headed to the door toward the back of the dome, which overlooked Atlas's second pond. I didn't have to turn the handle; the door was cracked open already, and I slid carefully inside. In the middle of the room was a dark oak desk, a metal chair, and a portal. On the desk was the nameplate: *Chairman Berea.* I didn't hear any sound coming from the room, so I walked in and closed the door lightly behind me. I began rummaging through the desk, careful not to displace anything but also hurrying as fast as possible.

There was nothing.

Nothing!

I looked through the rest of the office, in the closet and even under the rug. I walked back to the portal and hit the release button on the interchip drive. A small interchip slowly poked out from the base of the portal. I thought about turning the hologram screen on to watch whatever was on the chip, but I knew I had to get out of there before anyone found me. I grabbed the interchip and ran out of the office, heading down to the ground floor. I planned to leave Atlas from the south entrance, which was closer to the school. I wish I had known that before I came here because I would have entered that way as well. I dodged down to the ground level and headed toward the exit, but not before grabbing a handful of jelly beans at the café entrance.

I was heading back to the apartment, four hours later. The entire ordeal took much longer than I had expected. I hadn't gotten very far when I saw another girl eating jelly beans on a skateboard.

"Hey," she said, as she skated up slowly next to me.

"Hi," I replied, as I looked at her feet on the skateboard. Her sneakers looked so clean, like they were brand new. But it looked like the skateboard had been through hell and back.

"You're from Atlas?" she asked, looking down at my ID badge and then back up to me. I stuck the badge into my pocket.

"Um, yeah," I responded hesitantly. It wasn't exactly a lie. I was coming from Atlas.

"I've never seen you there before," she said. It was a statement, but she waited for an answer.

"I'm new."

"I'm Lonnie," she introduced herself, stepping off of her skateboard and lowering into a curtsy with one swift movement.

"El," I replied, and then I remember that my ID card had a large KM on it. "I mean Kel ... Kelly." She didn't seem to notice me stumble.

"You're a senior?" she asked.

I stared at her blankly.

"That's a student ID Pass. So, you're a student, right?"

"Oh yeah, senior," I winced. I had become such a liar that I sickened myself even though I knew deep down that there was no other way.

"I graduate this year," she said. "Thank God. I really think I'd kill myself if I had to spend another year at that school."

I just smiled politely at her.

"Where are you from?" she asked.

"Brooklyn," I answered instinctively.

She looked at me quizzically.

"I mean I live in Atlas now. Which is in Brooklyn," I added quickly.

She stared at me and continued to skate slowly.

"My grandmother is from Albany. There is an Elite Village called Babylon not far from there," I said. All those statements were true although none of them were relevant in the context of this conversation. With all the lies I had been telling lately, I didn't want it to become a habit that would be hard to break.

"Lucky. I would give anything to get away from Atlas," she said.

"What's wrong with Atlas?"

She scoffed and looked straight ahead. "That *is* the question."

I pondered that for a moment, but I didn't say anything in response.

"I can speak six languages and play eight musical instruments, and guess what?" she said, looking at me out of the corner of her eye.

"What?" I asked, intrigued.

"I want to fucking shoot myself!"

"Oh, I gasped taken aback. I hadn't expected an Elite to speak so vulgarly.

She shook her head as if to remove something that had landed on it, although I didn't see anything.

"Yeah well, I guess things can only be so perfect in Perfectville."

"Yeah, I guess so," I said. I could relate entirely to that expression. I had always said the exact opposite. *Things aren't so bad in the Badlands.*

"I guess it's probably the same in Babylon?"

I smiled.

"Why did you come to the outside?" she asked.

I didn't understand what she meant at first, so I just continued looking at her puzzled.

"Where are you going in the *slums*?" she clarified.

"Oh, I visit family … friends, really … that live out here."

She looked at me and hummed a deep questioning note.

"Well, I guess I'll see you around, then," she said, waving as she skated away.

We were outside of the Rec Center — a place set up by the community with computer portals, old fashioned board games, and vids. Mostly young kids and senior citizens hung out there. I wanted to ask her what she was doing there, but she was inside the building before I had a chance. It wasn't until I returned to the apartment that I remembered I was supposed to bring back coffee.

Shit. I thought about abandoning the coffee errand and blaming it on an outage at the Rations Center, but that would mean adding to my web of lies, plus Kai was already going to be upset about the ID Pass. A cup of coffee would do him well. I turned and headed for the Rations Center. It was about a fifteen-minute walk. Luckily there wasn't a line. I took out my ID Pass, and Kai's came out with it. I quickly shoved Kai's back into my pocket and looked around to make sure nobody had seen. A voice from behind me made me jump.

"Hey, Killer."

It was Pratt, the soldier I had met at the hospital shortly after the gas attack.

"What!" I blurted out, startled. "Oh, you. Hey." My voice sounded even ruder than I had expected. Pratt backed up slightly with his eyes widened. I guess even he was offended by my tone. Served him right. I didn't feel bad.

"Why so happy?" he asked with a scoff.

"I'm just in a rush," I responded while scanning my ID Pass at the turnstile.

The officer at the other end of the gate waited for the authoritative beeping sound and then waved me through to the center. I walked quickly toward the coffee.

"Big date to get to?" Pratt asked, following me into the warehouse.

I smirked. "Not even close."

He didn't say anything, but I thought I saw a hint of relief in his eyes.

"My friends are waiting for me," I said. We reached the beverage aisle, and I began filling up cups of coffee.

"Ah, I see. Well, let me help you," he said, he grabbed a cup from my hand and began filling it.

"No, really, I'm fine. I got the cup holder here," I said, as I filled the third and last cup and placed it into the holder.

"I'm heading that way, anyway. I'll walk you," Pratt said, adding one more cup to the tray and lifting it from the table. I looked at the extra cup.

"That one is for me. I'm walking that way, anyway," he repeated.

"But I didn't say which way I was going," I said, cocking my head to the side.

He just shot me a crooked smile and started walking toward the exit. It figured that on the day that I just wanted to be left alone, everyone I encountered wanted in on it. We headed down the street toward the apartment. I didn't mind the company. He held the coffee tray in one hand.

"Nothing beats the fall," he beamed, taking a deep breath in and exhaling loudly. It was early September, and the leaves had just begun to change color. He took one of the coffees out of the holder and took a sip. I sniffled and wiped my nose. There were a lot of things I put up with and even made the best out of, but I didn't like being cold.

"It's what comes after that I don't like," I said, grabbing one of the coffees.

"What? Old Man Winter? Why does he bother you?" Pratt asked grinning. "The cold weather is all the better to start a fire, drink some cocoa, and cuddle up with a book."

"You read?" I asked, surprised. It wasn't until after the words escaped my mouth that I realized how insulting they must have sounded. "I'm sorry, I didn't mean it to sound like that."

Based on the look on Pratt's face he didn't seem to take offense.

"I dabble in it," he smirked. "I think people see the guns, the camo, and the rugged good looks and assume

I sit around eating bananas and picking bugs out of my hair all day."

"I shrugged and smiled back at him.

"I like history and science," he continued. "I'll read anything I can get my hands on about culture and society, especially ancient societies."

"You have limited options, then," I said. The Elites had banned many works of literature and history that they had deemed offensive. You would be lucky to find mention of the Civil War of the 1860s in any textbook.

Pratt smiled.

"What?" I asked.

"I'll have to show you my library one day."

I looked at him quizzically. He pulled a book out of his jacket. I had never seen it before.

"What is this?" I asked as I opened it and scanned the pages.

"Read it. I think you'll like it."

I took the book and put it in my messenger bag.

"So, what's on the agenda for today?" he asked.

"It's just me and my friend, Kai. We're cleaning." That was the best I could come up with at the time. Pratt looked down at the two cups of coffee still in the holder.

"He drinks a lot of coffee," I added quickly.

After what felt like an eternity, we arrived at the apartment.

"Well, thanks for walking me home," I said with artificial cheer. I reached out to grab the coffees from Pratt's hands, but he didn't move. I stood in front of the door with my arms extended to receive the coffees, but instead, Pratt raised his eyebrows and headed into the building.

"It's getting cold out here," he said casually as he walked past me.

Figured.

I proceeded down to the shelter with Pratt following close behind me. Before I had a chance to announce

Pratt, I noticed Gianna standing in the middle of the room with her top off.

"Whoa!" Pratt turned to the side.

Feeling confused, I looked at Kai who was sitting not far across from her. Lee was there, as well. Gianna walked over to the cot where her shirt was casually thrown and began to put it back on.

"What's happening here?" I asked Kai.

"Nothing," Kai responded. "Gianna just wanted to show us her wounds."

"Her wounds?" I asked. I hadn't recalled her having any injuries on her torso, and Kai looked entirely too guilty to be looking at *wounds*. Not to mention Lee was smiling ear to ear.

Typical.

I looked around the room for Billy and saw him napping on the corner cot.

I roughly placed the coffee down on the table spilling some while staring directly at Kai. He looked awkwardly at the ground.

Then he glanced up and saw Pratt.

"What's he doing here?" Kai asked, suddenly aggressive.

"Well someone had to help El with the coffees considering you were busy looking at *wounds*." Pratt mimicked while winking at Kai. It was clear Pratt enjoyed provoking him.

The cot Kai was sitting on flew back as he stood up quickly. "She just lost someone to the goddamned Forces! Have some respect!"

The look on Pratt's face changed from cool and confident to stoic.

"Yeah, you have nothing to say now, do you?" Kai continued. I could tell he was looking for a fight.

"We aren't doing this right now," I scolded, putting my hands up in Kai's direction. "How can I see what is on this?" I took the interchip out of my pocket and held it out in front of me. They all stared at the interchip in my hand.

"What is that?" Kai asked.

"It's from Mr. Berea's office. I found it in his portal station." I braced myself for the reaction. Kai narrowed his eyes.

"You took my ID pass?" Kai asked angrily.

I nodded.

"What were you looking for at the Charter School?" Pratt asked.

"I'm not sure," I said. "But it may be on this chip."

"There is a portal station at the Rec Center," Kai offered. "Maybe I can get us onto a secure network from there."

"Those stations are monitored. If you try to tamper with them, they'll have Forces outside in less than five minutes. I have a portal station at my office that is undetectable," Gianna said. We all looked over at her. She had chugged her coffee and was standing up by the stairs.

"It's in my office down in the city by the old Trade Center."

Her office was eight subway stops away, and quite a walk from the last stop. If we could find our way there unnoticed, we could watch the interchip, and Gianna could create a broadcast to report the findings to the world. I still wasn't sure if she was ready to go on such a hike, but her theatrics with Kai, while I was away, made me care a little bit less. It was easy to see that Gianna was hungry for male attention and since she had been alone with Kai in the shelter on numerous occasions, I was certain that they had at least kissed, possibly more than that.

"We have to travel there without being seen," I said. "If the Forces find out what we are doing they'll likely kill us."

"Pratt, you have a car, don't you?" Kai asked.

"We can't take a car to Manhattan. There are cameras everywhere. The government would see a car on the radar immediately," Pratt answered.

"Well, there are no subways that go there directly," Kai said.

"Not directly, no, but I know a way," Pratt responded.

We followed Pratt to the subway, boarded, then exited at the Brooklyn Bridge and walked the length of it.

"Why don't we just take the F line?" Lee asked.

"Those lines are watched by the Forces. No direct lines to the Tower are left unguarded. We can take the C line to the corner of City Hall and then we will have to walk a few blocks from there. We can walk underground … there is an underground route that comes up right by the old Trade Center. We will only have to walk an avenue above ground from there," Pratt said.

"And how is it you know all of this?" Kai asked suspiciously.

"I was in the military," Pratt responded.

"Are you still in the military?" Kai asked aggressively. He turned to us. "How do we know we can trust him? He could be leading us right to the Forces."

We all stopped moving and looked at one another. Pratt noticed the hesitation. He turned to look at me and then addressed us as a group.

"I *was* in the military. I know where the Forces are stationed. You can come with me or not. If you want to see what's on the interchip, then you must come with me. If you don't, then don't. This is like herding cats."

I could see that he was becoming irritated by Kai's accusations.

"It's fine, Kai," I said. "I trust him." Kai looked at me warily, but eventually, he softened his stance and agreed to follow Pratt.

We reached the building but not without several close calls. Pratt was right about the location of almost every station security officer, but there were a few stray Elites that we had to avoid. We turned the corner and approached the building where Gianna had her remote office. She used her ID Pass to unlock the door and allow us access. There was no security officer at the front entrance. In fact, the building was surprisingly empty.

"Where is everyone?" I asked.

"This building used to be a hub full of reporters running in and out. Multiple stations used it as a remote office, but over time it has dwindled. Now, I'm lucky if I see one or two other reporters here," Gianna said.

"That's a good thing for us right now," Pratt said. "Let's move."

We wasted no time hurrying swiftly to the fourth floor and closing the door behind us as we entered the office. We put the interchip into the portal and watched as the footage began.

There were experiments, all right. Delancey, the director of the hospital, and a group of people in white lab coats were training Sleepers to speak and act like they were awake. The researchers had scripts that they would make the Sleepers recite, offering rewards for good performance. It was like watching monkeys being trained. The researchers were teaching the Sleepers to act as doctors, donors, celebrities, and TV reporters. They were creating puppets.

"Dear God," Lee cried.

We watched the footage in silence. I had expected something terrible to be on the interchip, but this was an abomination.

"No matter what happens to us, we need to get this out to the public," I stressed.

"There is a lock on the chip. I can't upload it to the network from here," Gianna said.

Pratt was staring at the portal screen in complete silence with his eyebrows deeply furrowed and his arms crossed.

"Did you know anything about this?" Kai pressed Pratt with his familiar accusatory tone.

Pratt glared at him from the corner of his eye, and then he uncrossed his arms and walked toward the window.

"Look, we don't have time to discuss this here," I said. "Chances are the Forces are looking for Gianna and Billy right now, and they could have seen her swipe her ID Pass to get into the building. Kai, you can break the lock on the interchip, can't you?"

Kai hopped onto the computer and began entering codes to try to get around the network's security system.

"It's going to take me a minute," Kai confirmed, as his fingers worked hastily away at punching in a series of codes.

"We don't have a minute." Pratt spat the words out of his mouth as he was looking out of the window at something. Gianna and I walked over to see what he was looking at. There were four large black trucks with tinted windows heading our way.

"We have to move!" Pratt said hastily.

Kai pushed one last button. "Done," he said, closing the portal and taking out the interchip.

We followed Pratt down the stairs and out of the building through the back alley. Across the street, there was a dormant subway station. We approached it, and Pratt lifted the yellow tape that blocked off the entry.

"Are you serious?" Gianna asked.

Certain subway lines hadn't been used in over a decade. The abandoned lines found new purpose as a home for crime, addicts, and criminals. The homeless had found their way into it years ago, and it was common knowledge not to enter.

"Ladies first," Pratt said, gesturing for Gianna and me to hurry inside.

We all ducked under the yellow caution tape and proceeded down the steps to the dark subway. It was the old A-line, it would take us out by the Brooklyn Bridge. The filth down in that tunnel even exceeded the back alleys of our Division. Sewage, rats, and debris of all sizes cluttered the passageway. The smell brought me back to the fifth day in the shelter before we began emptying the waste bucket. I tried to take the smallest breaths possible.

We followed Pratt through the tunnels for what seemed like an eternity. There were people down there; some were sleeping, but some called out to us. Some even looked like they wanted trouble. Then we came upon a man who was approaching us quickly. Kai broadened his shoulders, while Lee and I each took a fighting stance, as well. Gianna stood behind us with Billy.

"Hey, Pratt," the man said. He was wearing a shoulder holster.

"Donavan," Pratt responded. They embraced.

"Who are they?" the man asked warily.

"This is El Logan and her friends ... Kai, Lee, Gianna, and Billy. Everyone, this is Donavan."

"You coming in?" Donavan asked.

Donavan was a tall, slender, well-built man who carried himself in a militant manner. His blue eyes didn't match his dark complexion, and he spoke with a subtle Caribbean accent.

We walked into a small door off the side of the passageway that opened up into a large room, a spellbinding room. You could easily fit a hundred people in there. It was lit brightly with ceiling chandeliers and overhead lamps. The smell that lingered out in the tunnel only five feet away was no longer present once we closed the door. The stone walls were painted a golden color, illuminating the room. I could see now that in Donavan's holster was a handgun engraved with the words "Desert Eagle." A couch and a vid were off to the left, with a pool table and dartboard off to the right. In the center was a large table surrounded by chairs. In the back there appeared to be beds and curtains.

"What is this place?" I asked.

"We call it the Bedrock. It's a hideout," Pratt replied.

"Who knows about it?" Kai asked.

"Just us and now ... you. Let's keep it that way," Pratt said sternly.

We remained there until we thought the coast was clear, and then we exited the subway tunnel at Prospect Park and walked aboveground the rest of the way. We said our goodbyes to Gianna and Billy. Kai handed the interchip to Gianna.

"You'll be able to upload this to One Network now. You just need to find a portal that isn't monitored," he said.

"There is one at our sister station in Westchester. Hiyme's brother has a house there, too. We will be safe there," Gianna asserted.

"I'll take you there," Pratt said.

Gianna nodded.

"Good luck," I said to her. I kneeled down and gave Billy a hug.

Pratt's car was parked in front of our building. I walked over to it with him to thank him and say goodbye. He handed me another book out of his glove box.

"You can't build a future without knowing the past," he declared before climbing in.

I read the title aloud. *"Common Sense* by Thomas Paine."

Chapter Eight

Winter had passed, and so did spring. I had spent my time building a network of small communities that worked together in a barter and trade system. Doing so was dangerous because it lessened the people's dependence on the government, and that was unacceptable. We all understood this. I easily would be punished by death if I was caught, but we stayed hidden and kept a low profile.

People heard about our activities through word of mouth and began to call it the Laissez-Faire. It was a simple premise—Free Trade. A former owner of a barbershop in the outskirts of the Division who recently required medical care in his home offered to give Theo and Kai a shave and a haircut in lieu of payment. Another woman and her sister offered to clean my father's apartment as payment. A shoemaker who I had examined and treated for lice made Lou a pair of leather boots. Then there was a family with no lights in their home, so I introduced them to a man who made candles. In return, the family offered him cucumbers and tomatoes from their garden.

It was a simple system of barter and trade, but it worked. We didn't need to go to Rations Center for food and supplies, so we began going less and less. We realized that we could grow our food locally, make our own clothing, and trade it at fair value for other goods and services. The system ran all the way north to the upper Catskill region, and some traders were as far west as Michigan. We heard of other communities who were following in our footsteps and working on local networks themselves. We had a plan to bring the smaller networks together and make one larger system. Our main priority was to irrigate clean water out to the driest regions of the Southwest where people were unable to grow their own crops. People were calling it my movement, but I didn't feel that way. It was a team effort. Without the Hunters, the Gangsters, the Westerners, and all the others who participated in the Laissez-Faire, we wouldn't have had a movement at all.

The Hunters came from upstate New York. They had built a community they called New Hudson along the river that stretched from what used to be upper Westchester County all the way to the Catskills. The group was diverse in everything except for the fact that they lived off the land. They didn't use the Rations Centers at all; rather they lived quietly undetected by the government in small sub-villages throughout their community. Their leader was a man named Conan. He was a six-foot five-inch-tall red-haired burly man. He and his wife had six sons and a daughter, each of who lived in varying villages throughout New Hudson. Before the gas attack, Conan was a federal corrections officer who was ready to retire and head down south for easier living. When the attack occurred, he and his men cleared out the armory at the prison.

Summer was in full bloom, and Kai and I were heading home. It had been a long day of visiting the homes of people who needed medical care but who were scared of admitting themselves to the hospital. We brought water, medical supplies and information about our network directly to them. We hadn't yet reached the Rations Center that was in the center of the Division when we saw a rally taken place in the middle of the street. A large group of people had congregated around a speaker standing on a podium. I glanced over the crowd.

"You think they're rallying for more rations?" I asked Kai.

He shrugged his shoulders. We had seen protests over rations in the past, and they never ended well. Most of the time the organizers would simply go missing. The man at the podium was brave, whoever he was. I noticed Lonnie, the girl I met at the Elite Village, in the crowd and started over to her.

"Come on, Kai. I want to introduce you to someone."

I had been hanging out with Lonnie regularly, but she hadn't met my friends. I had admitted everything to her about being a Hoodlum and stealing an ID Pass. She wasn't mad at me for lying to her. In fact, she thought it was pretty cool. She was an Elite, but she was against everything that they stood for, which was a dangerous viewpoint to have.

"Kai, this is Lonnie. Lonnie, Kai," I said.

"Lonnie?" Kai asked, taken aback.

"Kai Maxwell?" Lonnie asked, craning her neck to get a better look at him. "So, your grandfather didn't cut you up into tiny pieces and hide your body in the rationed food."

"Wait, what?" I asked, looking at Kai for answers. He didn't have time to respond because just then we were interrupted.

"Ladies and gentlemen, there she is!" the speaker at the podium yelled into the microphone. "There is El! El Logan, come up here and tell us more about your plan to reconstitute this fallen haven!"

I was stunned. *This man recognized me?* That wasn't necessarily a good thing considering I was trying to keep a low profile. I nervously looked around the crowd. A lot of people were staring at me at this point. I felt my heart pound.

"This desolate concrete encampment of crime and hunger!" the man at the mic continued. "Tell us how you plan to restore mankind's faith in the American Dream! Come on up, El!"

I looked at Kai wide-eyed. *Is it too late to run?*

"You don't have to El, we can leave," he whispered, reading my thoughts.

I had never spoken at a rally before. I wasn't even sure what the man was talking about. *Reconstituting the haven of fallen ... what?*

Reluctant wasn't even the word to describe my thoughts at that moment. I looked over at Lonnie who was smiling at me from ear-to-ear.

"Go!" she cried, as she chortled. I hunched over slightly and felt my face squeeze smaller, perhaps in an attempt to hide.

"I can't," I said.

"You don't even know what people are saying, do you?" Lonnie asked. "Everyone claims you're running against the Elite in the election. They see what you've been doing here in Brooklyn, and it's spreading across the state, El."

I shook my head. "No, I never said that."

Lonnie nodded and gave me a gentle shove forward, but in my tensed state it was enough to send me into a stumble. Kai caught and steadied me.

"You don't have to do anything you don't want to do," he reiterated. "You do realize how easy it would be for me to pick you up and run out of here, don't you?" He was joking, but I knew he would actually do it if I asked. I was grateful.

"I want to speak," I sighed. "I just don't know if I can."

All traces of humor left his face when he listened to those words. He looked me in the eyes.

"Well, of course, you can," he said. "You can do anything."

It wasn't his words that I needed to hear, but it was how positively sure he was when he said them that gave me the courage to face the man at the podium. I nodded up to him.

"Yes! Here she comes!" the orator's voice echoed through the street.

"Okay," I sighed, taking a deep breath and walking toward the podium with Kai at my side.

As we began to walk towards the stage, Kai gave a quick look back over his shoulder and whispered to me, "You know that is Lonnie Berea, right?"

"Berea?" I asked.

"Yeah, Johan Berea's daughter."

I thought about the implications. She was the daughter of the chairman of the Elite school, the school she despised, the school we were trying to bring down. That girl must *really* dislike her father.

"We went to school together," Kai said. "I was a few grades older ... I think I was in fifth grade when she was in first grade, but I remember her well. Have you told her anything about what we are doing?"

"I don't think so," I said, trying to recall if I had. I remember her saying that she spoke six languages, hated Atlas, and liked my shoes. Nothing about espionage or human experiments.

"No, I didn't tell her anything," I maintained. "But Kai, I don't think she's one of them."

"She lives there. She's one of them," Kai assured me.

I heard the man at the podium call my name again. The crowd was probably fifty to sixty people deep. As we continued to make our way through the swarm of people many cheered, touching my arm as I passed, clapping wildly. Not everyone appeared so thrilled, however. Some leaned toward one another and whispered. Some even looked angry, shooting me sour faces as I passed. I began to feel nervous again. A hand suddenly reached out and grabbed mine. I looked up and instantly locked eyes with the hand's owner. *Pratt.*

"Hey, you," he smiled, his eyes piercing mine.

"Hey," I replied with unexpected relief. His gaze held me in place longer than I had intended. His hazel eyes were stunning against his olive skin, and not even the dark baseball cap he wore could disguise that. He made the crowd disappear with his smile.

"Better you than me. I have stage fright," he said, nodding towards the stage with a smirk.

I tried to smile back but I couldn't. It wasn't stage fright for me; I didn't know if I would be able to be what everyone expected me to be.

"This doesn't make sense. I don't know what I'm doing," I confessed. I searched his face for the answer that he always seemed to have and landed on his smile.

"I think sometimes it takes time for things to make sense," he winked. "I'll be right here. Your own personal cheerleader."

I caught Kai's dirty look at Pratt. Kai placed his hand on the small of my back to continue our walk. I knew he likely wanted to cut our conversation short. I turned back to Pratt and smiled.

Kai walked with me all the way to the stage. Then he stayed behind as I began my ascent up the narrow steps to the podium.

The stage was small and makeshift and was adorned with a wooden podium that came about waist high. The speaker held the mic in his hand. The amplifiers were set at the far left and right corners of the stage pointing outward. I wondered how far the sound projected. I looked up and saw people in apartment buildings, standing on fire escapes, and on the rooftops. The speaker handed me the microphone, and I swallowed hard.

"Hello," I uttered, the microphone close to my mouth. The amplifiers screeched. I took a pause that was too long for most people.

The crowd shuffled uncomfortably in the silence.

"I am—" I began. "I have … I mean, think." I stumbled to form a sentence. I wasn't sure what words to say first. I wanted to say them all, yet they wouldn't form in my mind. I started to have trouble breathing. My hands and voice began to shake while my body temperature rose, causing sweat to form on my brow.

The people were staring at me in silence. Then, whispers became louder and turned into groans and jeers, and some people started to leave. I scanned the audience while I wiped my brow with the back of my hand. I locked eyes with Kai, and he parted his mouth as if to say something. I knew what he would say. *You are great, and you can do anything you put your mind to.* I wished I could be the person he thought I was.

My eyes continued to scan the crowd. The faces, some familiar, some not, all looked alike from up here. The small differences in skin tone, hair color, and features were not visible from up on the podium. They were not individuals to me. They were united. They were one.

I took a breath and tried to imagine myself in the crowd along with them. *We are all in this together.*

My eyes locked on the most beautiful and familiar eyes. I caught my sister's gaze. *Lou Lou.*

I was twelve when she was born. I carried her around like she was my own; bathed her, read to her, rocked her to sleep.

"Hi," Lou signed.

I signed "Hi" back. I propped the mic into its holder so I could use my hands. Then I spoke and signed at the same time.

"A lot of you don't remember because you're too young. I've seen many things change throughout my life. I was two when the Elites took power, and things weren't too bad at first. I remember a time before the Divisions, when I was five or six, when things were happy … we were happy. Our parents had work, and children rode their bikes. But we went from being free to being scared. But we don't have to be afraid because no one can hurt us with our backs together. We can keep a lookout for each other.

"We are a nation of individuals, and each one has their own talents and skills to contribute to society. We don't need to be content with what we are handed by the Elites. They give us so little, and what they give us is poison. Yet we come running back for more, barely getting by. We see our homes crumbling, and our families dying. We are dependent upon a government who purposefully holds us down, while the Elites stay safely tucked away in the Villages unaffected by the turmoil that they created, and that we must suffer through daily.

"But we outnumber them ten-fold. We can make our own wealth and build our own houses ... with our own hands. We can help one another. I know it's possible because I've seen it. It's time we freed ourselves from the constraints the Elites have placed on us. It's time we come together as individuals and allow free trade and private sectors. It's time we have less government and more freedom. It's our time. It's our time!"

The crowd started chanting, "It's our time! It's our time!"

I looked over the crowd of people cheering, they were old and young, black and white. They were a sea of individuals screaming just to be heard.

"It's our time," I sighed.

Chapter Nine

That was it. My words spread like wildfire.

All twelve Divisions in Brooklyn had heard of me, and they began calling what we were doing the Laissez-Faire Movement. Posters began popping up with my face on them, and I was recognized walking down the street.

I had guessed that the Elites wouldn't be happy about all of this, but I also guessed that they wouldn't be too afraid of me. I was just one young woman from Brooklyn. If it weren't for the Elites, I wouldn't have even been eligible to run for office. The Constitution used to require a person to be thirty-five or older to run for office, but when the Elites modified the Constitution that was all cleared out. The 12th and 22nd Amendments were completely removed to allow Torrent to remain president for the last twenty years.

Anyway, they probably thought I would just crash and burn, but that didn't seem to be the case. With each rally, the crowds grew, and more and more posters and signs of my face popped up. That caused the Elites to alert government officials to keep an eye on me.

I had just left the Bedrock. We had been slowly stocking food, medicine, and weapons there in case we needed a place to hide out. I was heading to meet Kai and Lonnie at the apartment when a group of teenagers on the Brooklyn Bridge noticed me.

"We are the Laissez-Faire!" one of them shouted.

"I'm glad to hear that! It's nice to meet you." I spoke with them for a short while.

They asked about the plans we had for our movement and how it would be implemented. I began to explain the policy of free trade and capitalism.

I heard the sirens before I saw the lights. The group dispersed swiftly. I figured the cops would drive right past me off to some accident or emergency, but the car slowed and the driver rolled down his window.

"Look what we have here. If it's not the famous El Logan?" he asked. His mustache was large, larger than it needed to be, and it hung down at the tips past his narrow chin in a mangy looking way.

I stood and looked at him and the cop in the passenger seat in the eyes. My father had taught me how to interact with the police. He taught me to have respect and comply with their commands.

"Hello, officers. Is there a problem?" I asked.

The officer driving put the car in park and opened his door. I saw the passenger exit the car, as well.

"If by 'problem' you mean *you*. Then yeah, we have a problem," he said.

"I'm sorry. I don't understand," I said, backing up slightly.

"You don't?" the other cop asked. "That's funny because the law clearly states that any public assembly that calls to dismantle an authoritative body is highly illegal in all Divisions." He adjusted his pants over his round belly.

"I understand, and I apologize," I said. "I wasn't trying to assemble. I was just walking home." The cop licked his lips and proceeded to stare at me, tapping his foot impatiently. I took this as a request for more information, so I continued talking. "The group of people I was talking to was just asking me for directions," I lied.

"Directions?" the cop mocked. "Well you see, we got asked to do something also, honey." He walked closer to me. Both cops were well past my comfort zone at this point.

"We were asked to bring you in if we spotted you out and about holding one of your illegal assemblies," the cop with the mustache said.

"Oh, no. I wasn't," I began.

"Oh, but you were," the smaller, rounder cop asserted. He lifted his hand and combed his fingers through my hair. "We were instructed from the highest authority to bring you down." He paused and examined my body. "Bet you look a whole lot sweeter when you're brought down."

"She's prettier in person. I think she'll look good in stripes," snickered the other cop. Their toothy grins and their sinister cackles sent chills straight up my spine. "Turn around. Let's get these cuffs on you."

"No, please!" I looked around and thought about running, but where could I go? I looked over the side of the bridge. There was only one option. My breath was loud in my ears, and I knew what I had to do.

I had to jump.

Then I saw more lights. As if these men, if they could be called men, needed any backup. The car coming toward us looked a little different than the cop car, however. The two men turned to look, as well.

It was my chance to jump, but I hesitated. It was the sheriff. He stopped right in front of us. The two cops continued to look his way. His window was already down, and his elbow was hanging out of it. He exhaled smoke from the cigarette hanging out of his mouth. "Get lost," the Sheriff ordered.

"But, Sheriff—" one officer began.

"Did I stutter?" he asked, putting the car into park.

The two officers didn't give me a second look. They headed back into their car and drove away like nothing had happened. I stood very still, my eyes wide and my arms hanging tight at my sides, as I thought about what could have happened. I looked at the Sheriff.

"I'm Sheriff Chaplin," he stated, speaking clearly and confidently. "Get in the car." I didn't move. He threw his cigarette over the bridge railing, and I watched the light fall to the water. "I'll take you home."

I climbed into the back seat. He looked at me in the rearview mirror. "You didn't have to sit back there."

I still didn't speak.

"You might have noticed that there are people out for your head. The government wants you taken out. You need protection ... people you can trust. Do you understand?"

I looked at his eyes in the rear-view mirror. I nodded.

He was heading in the right direction to my home.

"How do you know where I live?" I asked.

He gave me a cynical look in the mirror and looked back at the road.

"Why?" I asked. He looked back at me. "Why do they want me taken out?"

"Cause you're a threat," he declared. "Look what you've done ... what you're *doing*."

"I'm not trying to hurt anyone."

"That's just it ... you're not. And that's why I'm taking you home, and that's why you're going to find yourself some protection."

We pulled up to the apartment.

"Now, I'm only *one* sheriff. There are twelve in Brooklyn and a hundred more in New York, New Jersey, and Connecticut. I can tell you we aren't all against you. Trust no one in the government. They're working for one person."

"Don't you work for her, too?"

"I work to protect the Division. My father and his father before him did the same."

"Will you be in trouble for this?"

"Don't worry about me. I answer to only one person, and it isn't anyone around here."

As he put the car into park, he lit up a new cigarette. He opened the door from the outside for me, I had forgotten that I had locked myself in there like a real criminal.

"I know you think anyone who passes the aptitude test is stupid," he said. I opened my mouth to protest. "The thing with the Elites is that they like to play mind games. Plant ideas in your head. They'll use your words against you and find ways to turn the people against you, too. Surround yourself with people you trust. No one wins a battle alone."

"Have a good night," he uttered, and he drove away.

So, Torrent had her Mules on me like glue. Scarier than that was the thought of the Elk. He was the man who worked for the president, did her dirty work. I had never seen him, but I had heard stories, and I knew I needed a team of my own. I told Theo what had happened, and he began recruiting a team for my protection.

Chapter Ten

"Fishing," Kai grunted for the hundredth time. He shook his head. "Why would you say that? I've never even hooked a worm, never mind caught a fish."

Dad had been questioning me about Kai's fishing trip, and I couldn't avoid dinner with my family much longer. It was five in the morning. Pratt looked on as a sleepy Kai, and I loaded up Pratt's truck with a worn net we had found in a storage unit of the apartment, a bucket, and a makeshift fishing rod made from a broomstick, some string, and a hook. He had offered to help us city folk.

"Well, I had to say *something*," I responded. "We can still say they weren't biting and just bring over the deer the Hunters gave us. Dad said Lou likes venison."

"Right, and have your father think I can't fish," Kai said.

"Where are your supplies?" I asked Pratt as I shoved the bucket deep into the empty flatbed of his truck.

Pratt raised his eyebrows and watched me struggle. "They're already up at the river," he said.

"The river? I thought we were going to Coney Island?" Kai questioned, turning abruptly to Pratt.

"You want trout? We need a river," Pratt said, closing the bed of his truck. "We're going to the Amawalk."

"The Amawalk?" I asked.

"It's a river in a town called Somers in Westchester County," Pratt replied.

"Westchester? That's over an hour north!" Kai said.

"It's an hour. And if you want to catch trout you have to fish where there are trout," Pratt said. "Plus, you don't want to eat anything that comes out of the city." He stuck out his tongue and wrinkled his nose. He was right about that. We had all seen what went into the water around us and it wasn't anything that you wanted to ingest.

The drive was quiet. Kai fell asleep in the back seat, and Pratt was tapping his finger on the steering wheel to some music I had never heard before. I stared out the window. As we left the city, the houses and people became more and more scarce. It was hard to believe that not too long ago in the vast empty space were populated towns with houses, shops, and restaurants. Now it all appeared to be one large ghost town with a hopeless few left just barely getting by. I must have fallen asleep because when I opened my eyes, we were driving down a bumpy driveway with a small green house in the distance. "Where are we?" I asked, rubbing my eyes.

"We're here," Pratt announced.

The green house was pushed back along a quarter mile driveway of broken cement and pebbles. The house was small, but well-kept and surrounded by woods. The word I would use to describe it was *ordinary*. The beige shutters were closed, and a porch that extended the entire circumference of the home was decorated with stone and wooden fixtures, two rocking chairs, and a bench. A welcome mat sat at the front door. The surrounding woods were dense, and leaves covered all that the eye could see.

Pratt parked the car, and we climbed out. I could hear the rush of the river, and the smell of autumn leaves was potent as we walked up the three steps to the front porch. I watched as Pratt grabbed a key from under a stone frog, which stood next to the bench.

"Original spot for a hidden key," Kai said sarcastically.

Pratt walked back down the steps into the front yard while Kai and I stood on the porch. I glanced over at Kai who just shrugged and looked back over at Pratt.

"Should we follow you?" Kai asked.

"Nope," Pratt responded as he walked over to a tree that stood off to the right of the driveway. He reached his arm deep inside a hollowed opening and pulled out a small box. He opened it with the key to reveal another key. It was such an original hiding spot that even Kai had to smile. He took that key and came back up the steps, unlocking the door and top bolt.

Pratt walked in, and we followed right behind him. We were in the living room. There was an old grandfather clock, a coffee table, and a beige couch on top of wood floors. A stack of old newspapers cluttered the coffee table. I noticed that there was no vid or portal.

"Whose house is this?" I asked.

"Mine," Pratt replied as we walked through the living room and toward the kitchen. The yellow wallpaper was peeling in some spots, and the round kitchen table had only one chair. Pratt opened a closet door.

"I thought you told me you were from Division 4," I said.

"I told you I *lived* in Division 4," Pratt responded. "I grew up here. Not much to it. Two bedrooms down that way, a bathroom off the kitchen here. You saw the living room." I looked at the walls, but no family photos were hanging, or any photos for that matter.

"Well, are we taking a tour through your childhood, or are we fishing?" Kai asked seemingly annoyed by the walk down memory lane.

Pratt ignored the comment. The closet door he had opened led into a walk-in pantry. Pratt stepped inside and pulled the string that hung next to the light bulb on the ceiling, illuminating the room. The shelves inside the pantry were scarcely stocked with appliances and what appeared to be garbage, empty cans, and plastic bags. He moved the far back shelf entirely to expose a trapdoor.

A cellar.

He pulled the door open, generating a cloud of dust that flew up in my face. I coughed. Pratt descended first, followed by Kai, and then me. Upon reaching the bottom of the steps, Pratt flicked on another light revealing an arsenal of weapons, tools, and what especially caught my eye, books.

"Wow!" Kai exclaimed, his eyes scanning the rifles and magazines.

"This is the cellar," Pratt announced proudly.

I was already at the books. There were three shelves as tall as the room itself, filled with some books I had never seen or even heard of before. They seemed to be organized into categories: History, Fiction, and Fantasy.

I looked over the History section. *The Civil War: A Narrative, Volume I, Fort Sumter to Perryville. Washington: A Life.* I had heard of both the war and the man. My nan and my school had taught me very different accounts of both. *These must be the books that Nan used to read growing up.* I walked over to the Fiction section.

"*To Kill a Mockingbird?* Why do they kill the mockingbird?" I asked.

"It's a good read," Pratt responded with a smile.

"Where did you get all of these books?" I asked.

"They've been in the family for years. Most were my fathers and some were my brother's. I've added to the collection since."

"Since?"

"Since they died."

"Did they die in the attack?" I asked. My question may sound crude, but it was normal to ask considering most people did die in the gas attack.

Pratt didn't hesitate. "No."

I blinked and decided to not ask the follow-up question. I looked at some of the other titles: *The Great Gatsby, The Catcher in the Rye, Killing Lincoln.* There was one I was familiar with: *The Holy Bible*. Nan had told me about it. I grabbed it and looked at Pratt.

"Can I read this while we are out fishing?"

He nodded.

Fishing rods were in the corner. These were *real* fishing rods, not the broomsticks with string and hooks that Kai and I had brought. Pratt grabbed three and shoved them into Kai's arms. He also grabbed a knife, a bucket, a shovel, and a box of some sort of accessories. Then he turned to us.

"You ready to go fishing?"

We headed to the dock behind the house. I held the two buckets. It wasn't a far walk, but navigating through the leaves and downed tree limbs made it feel further. When we got to the dock, Pratt took his shovel and dug into the soil. He began picking out worms and putting them into one of the buckets. Kai did the same. After they had a few worms stockpiled, Pratt grabbed one and began to hook it to his line. Kai followed his lead.

"You should double hook that worm," Pratt said looking over at Kai's bait.

"It's fine," Kai declared defensively.

Pratt raised his brow and shrugged his shoulders, then headed down toward the water as Kai continued to fumble with his worm. Pratt waded into the shallow stream until he was about a foot deep, and then drew back his rod and cast it forward.

I found myself lost in my book. The Bible was longer than Nan had made it seem from her stories, and much more difficult to follow. I looked up, occasionally taking breaks from reading. Pratt stood casually tossing the line back and forth against the water. Kai looked a bit more awkward.

Kai and Pratt were opposites but still so much alike. They were good men with good hearts, that much I knew. They both had specific skill sets, which set them apart from the average man. Kai was great with portals, interchip programming, and anything to do with networks. Pratt was a pro at this fisherman thing, and he knew how to shoot and hunt. I guessed that had to do with his military training and perhaps his upbringing, based on the looks of this property.

Kai managed to hook his worm, and he waded into his own spot not too much further downriver from Pratt. Within five minutes, Pratt had caught a brown trout. Kai watched from the corner of his eye as Pratt took his fish off the hook and tossed it into the clean bucket. Kai licked his lips, pulled back his fishing rod, and then cast it forward with such force that he threw himself face-first into the river. He grumbled as the small current rolled him over. Shuffling to his knees, he searched for his rod.

I stood up. "Kai!" I exclaimed running toward the water. Pratt drew in his reel and hopped downriver to Kai's side. He bent to help pick him up, but Kai shook Pratt's hands off of him.

"I don't need your help," he cried sharply as he stood up wiping his hands on his jeans. Pratt reached down and picked up Kai's rod.

"Yeah, I see that," Pratt muttered, looking at Kai's bloodied hands.

Pratt handed Kai the rod he was using. "Try this one. It's hooked already."

Kai sighed deeply and grabbed it. It was clear that he was mustering up every bit of strength he had to keep his composure. He took a few steps forward and pulled back his arm to cast the line.

"More of a forty-degree angle," Pratt said. "You're not throwing a baseball. It isn't distance you're aiming for, 'Man of Steel.'"

Kai cracked a smile, he perceived Pratt's words as a compliment.

"Just hold it like this." Pratt demonstrated the stance. "And when you pull back, it's here you want to be."

Kai mimicked Pratt's stance and held the rod at the same angle.

"Now cast, but think only ten to fifteen feet and stay low. You're looking directly at the center of the water, and you want to stay right above the current." Kai nodded and pulled back his rod. He cast forward.

"Good. Now, back again," Pratt instructed. Kai pulled back and did it again. "Good!" Pratt said, reassuringly.

Kai began to look more confident. His shoulders eased then tensed up with each cast. "I think I got something!" I saw his line tug as he pulled the rod back and began to reel in his cast. Sure enough, a large brown trout came up with his next pull.

"Aha!" he shouted as he reeled it in.

"Pull it in!" Pratt encouraged.

"Look at the size of this sucker!" Kai proclaimed, proud of his accomplishment.

"That's big enough to feed an elephant! No need to stay and fish any longer, let's go home!" Pratt joked, as he turned and pretended to leave.

I smiled watching them. They were laughing *with* each other and not *at* each other. Pratt took the fish off of the hook for Kai and tossed it into the bucket. He grabbed another worm and hooked it for him. Kai watched carefully this time as Pratt double hooked the worm to keep it from falling off.

"Let's see if you can do that again," Pratt said. A confident grin spread across Kai's face.

We went home around noon with twenty fish. I read my book in the back seat the entire drive home. Kai and Pratt sat in the front and talked about fishing, the army, portals, and politics. We reached my father's apartment around two. Pratt unlatched the bed of his truck and handed Kai the bucket of fish, and then closed the bed and headed back to the driver's seat.

"You're staying for dinner, aren't you?" Kai asked.

"Oh, nah. I have stuff I have to do," Pratt lied, unconvincingly. "I have this thing I have to do ..."

Kai and I both looked at Pratt with pity.

"You're staying for dinner," Kai said firmly.

Pratt smiled and nodded. "Okay, I guess I am." He closed his truck door and walked inside with us.

I wasn't surprised that Dad and Pratt got along well. Dad reminisced with him about his old army days. Lou signed something to Pratt. He looked over at me.

"She says you're handsome," I said, batting my eyelashes. Lou laughed when she saw me relay the message to Pratt.

"Oh, I've been called a lot of things, but handsome isn't usually one of them. We're going to have to get her eyes checked out." He smiled.

Lou read his lips and laughed even louder.

Pratt talked to Nan about books and history.

"Do you know who Christopher Columbus is?" Nan asked, poking a fork in Pratt's direction. "Because I keep hearing that he is a war criminal, but I don't recall the war of 1492."

Pratt laughed, and they discussed the early Native American settlements, the pilgrims' migration to North America, and the violence that ensued both before and after the pilgrimage. They discussed the politics of immigration and the history of America itself. I could see Lou's eyes bright and wide as she read lips while she ate her fish. She had never seen a discussion like this before. A free and open discussion in which each person had the right to say what they wanted to say, object, and interject with counterarguments. We could be arrested for such talk.

After dinner, Pratt told my family that he enjoyed meeting them. I walked him to the door, while Kai, Dad, and Nan continued to talk.

"Thanks," I said. "For everything."

"You have a great family."

"They like you." I smiled. "Oh, let me go get your book," I said, turning back to the apartment.

"That's yours, now," he replied quickly before I could get too far. "You can't build a future without knowing the past." He smiled, and then he turned and headed into the hallway.

The next few days I made house calls to folks who were afraid to go to the hospital. I met a family whose youngest daughter was one of the sleeping. They had trained her to repeat phrases and actions to blend in when she was out in public. She had developed a sinus infection, which I treated with an antibiotic. She sat still during my examination, and when I stood up to leave the room, she thanked me for seeing her.

"Um, you're welcome," I replied. Then I turned to her parents. "You trained her to do that?"

"It's just repetition. She repeats what she hears, and we reinforce the behavior we want with treats," the mother said. Her thin fingers curled a strand of greying-blond hair that was hanging down by the side of her face.

The girl leaped off the bed and joined her older sisters who were playing a game on the floor in the den. I didn't question the parents on their decision to conceal their daughter's condition, nor did I judge them for it. They were aware that their daughter was a Sleeper and that the speech and behavior was nothing more than mimicry. They told me that they were waiting for a cure, and I didn't argue with that either.

At work the next day, I was stitching up a man's back, which had gotten sliced open in an alley fight. He had a lot of piercings and even more tattoos. An old lady in the bed next to him gave him a smile. She liked the tattoos. He smiled back. The next time I saw her, she had a huge neck tattoo, and she told me it was from his studio. She told me all about how she made him pasta, and explained to him, "This jar is the mushroom sauce, and this one is the one with the garlic. Don't forget, this one is spicy. Make sure you have toilet paper rations the day you eat that one!"

Conan and the Hunters visited with a truckload of rabbit fur and meat saying that they had heard I could help them find ammo. I introduced them to the BK12 who agreed upon a trade. The Hunters gave them one hundred pounds of rabbit meat, skin, and fur for five cases of .22 ammo.

"Salt that meat, keep it frozen, and you'll eat for a year," one of the Hunters told Theo and his friend, Sanzhar.

Conan thanked us, and I told him to spread the word about what we were doing, and I promised that I would tell other traders about them.

"We have a lot of meat and a lot of furs. We could use candles, cotton, and we always like bullets," Conan added with a grin.

I told Theo about the shoemaker, and I guessed the BK12 had taken the furs to them because the next time I saw the gang they were all decked out in fur-trimmed coats and boots.

One night Kai turned on the vid, and we sat in front of it to watch Gianna's newscast. Pratt had driven her to her brother's home outside the city where she would have been able to safely access the One Network with the interchip Kai had programmed. We sat anxiously, waiting to see Gianna come on screen. I reached down and grabbed Kai's hand tightly, and he squeezed mine back as the broadcast began. Gianna began her reporting, but something wasn't right. She began talking about the weather and traffic.

Then she announced, "All is well here in New York and across America."

Kai's face was long, and I imagined mine must have been, too. We couldn't be certain what had happened to her, but somewhere along the way, the Forces must have found Gianna and Billy. She was a Puppet, turned into a Sleeper and brainwashed to say whatever the government programmed her to say. We had no idea what that meant for her son.

Chapter Eleven

Lou had the vid on. She was watching some reality show with three sisters who were eating crab cakes in their Upper East Side penthouse.

"Have you ever tried those?" Lou signed to me.

"Crab cakes?" I signed.

Lou nodded.

"No."

Lou smiled and turned back to the vid. I walked over and turned it off. She looked at me and grunted.

"Well, it's garbage."

"Where do we get crab cakes?" she signed back.

"Not at the Rations Center," I smiled. "We would have to catch the crabs, make bread, then breadcrumbs, and mix it all together with some butter. That's a lot of work."

"Yeah, sounds like it."

"Want me to make some for your birthday this year?"

She smiled and nodded.

"I'll try my best." I pushed a strand of her light brown hair off her face.

I grabbed the remote and was placing it on top of the vid when it fired back on automatically. Before I could turn it off, I saw Torrent's face on the screen. There was a woman in a Logan and Co. T-shirt and cargo pants standing in the middle of a group of people.

I realized the woman was supposed to be me. She was laughing and taking food and clothing out of the hands of the people standing around her. Then celebrities and politicians came and beat the El character up and gave the people back their belongings. Everyone cheered. The singer, Addy Purdy, came on the air yelling, "Vote Torrent ... she's fighting for you to keep what's yours."

"What is this?" I asked aloud.

Lou groaned at my side. I was dumbfounded. It seemed like the Elites were fighting to keep what was theirs rather than campaign on facts. Addy Purdy came on screen again. "Hello, Divisions of all." She swished around her long blue hair with each syllable. "I am Addy Purdy, and I hope you stand with us in voting for President Torrent on Election Day! Take a look outside, my loves, here I am!" She blew a kiss to the screen, which exploded with digitized hearts as she winked and faded off camera.

I looked out the window as the ividcams popped on. They showed Addy Purdy's hologram dancing wearing an *I Love Torrent* t-shirt. She waved and blew kisses while pretending to interact with children who she really couldn't see since she was just a hologram. The young girls in the neighborhood and some boys were hanging out of their windows and gathering in the streets to watch.

She was the biggest celebrity of our time. Her natural brown hair was often dyed a different shade of neon. It was mostly young girls who admired her, but there were a handful of adults who considered her to be an icon, as well. She aligned herself with the Torrent political team early on in their administration, and the two went hand-in-hand. Purdy had homes in six of the Elite Villages throughout the States. She was in her mid-thirties but she was single, she had no children and was always dating a new celebrity. Last week she was dating Madeline Blu, a singer who fit more into the urban scene. Her music was about the struggles of Hoodlums and the hardships of life in the Divisions.

Meanwhile, she regularly flew on a private jet around the nation for luxury vacations and tours.

Addy had begun performing her latest hit called "I am a Cookie, Be my Milk." She put on a ridiculously enormous hat that stretched high and straight up. It was topped with a small figurine of Torrent.

Suddenly I heard sirens. Two cars pulled up out front of the apartment. They were blacked out jeeps with lights, so it was easy to recognize them as government vehicles. Two minutes later there was a knock at the door. I wondered what this could be about. I answered the door warily, certain to make sure that Lou was nowhere in sight. There were two men, one quite tall and thin and one rather short and very round. The pairing looked peculiar side by side, and I stared at them perhaps longer than appropriate. They spoke before I could say a word.

"Elisha Logan?" the large man asked.

"Yes?" I responded through the crack in the door.

"You are hereby summoned to Torrent Tower." He handed me a Tower ID card. "This will allow you access at noon tomorrow. Will you be needing a car?"

Torrent Tower. Torrent wants to meet me.

Perhaps she was finally coming around after all. If she wanted to meet me, then she probably was interested in hearing what I had to say, and if I could talk to her, I could tell her my ideas for implementing change in the Divisions. Perhaps this was the opportunity I had been waiting for.

"Um, yes. A car would be great. Thank you."

"Be outside at 11:45 a.m.," the smaller man announced.

Without another word they turned around and left.

I knew that this was my one chance to convince Torrent that I was serious about this election. I needed help, and I knew just who to call.

The following morning, I had Lonnie bring me over a skirt and heels. She did my makeup and hair and even painted my nails. For the first time in my life, I felt like a woman.

"There!" she exclaimed, pleased with her masterpiece.

I stared in the mirror, assessing what was just done to me. I reminded myself that in politics you had to look the part.

"Maybe she'll listen to me now that I look like one of them," I said, winking at Lonnie. She recognized that I was only kidding. I knew very well that the Elites weren't all bad. Lonnie was one, and Kai had been one, too.

The next morning, I stood outside at eleven-thirty. The Mules were right on time, but they were different than the two who had come to see me the day before. I climbed into the limo. The drive to Manhattan took under twenty minutes, and the Mules drove in silence.

I looked out of the window to pass the time. There were no stationed soldiers or stone walls. The closest Elite Village was Spire, and that was over twenty miles away. The Tower was impossible to miss. It was the immaculate, gargantuan, and stark white building in the middle of the rubble. Many of the surrounding buildings had been demolished to make room for the president's "training fields" years ago. The area was used as a military base of sorts where newly recruited Mules were taught weaponry and combat skills.

When we finally reached the Tower, the driver pulled up to the front of the building and stopped the vehicle. I hesitated, but no one moved or spoke. I tried my hand at the door handle and was surprised when it opened. The trip to the Tower had felt so much like a ride in a police car that I expected the locks to be disengaged from the inside.

"Uh, thanks for the ride," I uttered, closing the door behind me.

I walked slowly to the entry doors, and before entering, I looked up at the massive structure before me. This was it—my first attempt at diplomacy. I swiped the ID Pass and saw the red lock turn green. The heavy doors opened to a grand lobby. It was everything I had thought it would be. A large marble statue of Torrent graced the center of the room along with holographic images of herself and her fellow Elites. What was more daunting were the Mules stationed everywhere. I walked apprehensively toward one of them, trying my best to appear poised.

"My name is Elisha Logan. I'm here to see President Torrent."

He glared at me from under his brow. "Follow me," he grunted.

I shadowed him into an elevator and up to the thirty-second floor. When the elevator stopped, and the doors opened, the man stayed inside. Bruna, Torrent's assistant, came into sight.

"Ms. Logan, such a pleasure to have you here. Please follow me." A painted smile lingered on her face.

"Thanks," I said, following her down the long hallway and into a large conference room. The window in the room extended the entire length of the twenty-five-foot table that was placed in the center. I stood mesmerized by the view of the entire city laid out down below.

"Have a seat!" Torrent exclaimed, startling me as she entered the room swiftly. I took a seat as she sat down beside Bruna across from me. They smiled at me as I looked back and forth between the pair. I smiled back while forcing myself to maintain eye contact with at least one of them. The silence became too uncomfortable to bear, so I spoke.

"Lovely view," I said, gesturing to the window.

"Isn't it?" Torrent asked. "Would you like to have a view like this?"

I glanced around, caught unaware by the question. "I wouldn't mind."

"We are willing to offer you a position here at the Tower."

"A position?" I asked, confused.

"Yes, a public relations position. You would be a government employee ... an Elite. Your family would have the option to move into Atlas Village, and your little sister, Louie, would attend Charter Atlas." She seemed proud of her offer.

Her assistant sat with the same smile still plastered on her face.

"Thank you for the offer, Madam President, but I am not looking for employment in your administration. I am running for president."

Torrent's smile faded. She looked sideways at Bruna who stood up and left the room.

It was just Torrent and me.

"Listen to me, and listen well. You're not going to be needed anymore. Your little show ... it's over. You're going to find a spot in some valley somewhere, and you are going to live and die there ... alone or with your family ... doesn't matter. Because *you* don't matter. But let me make one thing *very* clear. I hope you enjoyed the view from up here because you will never see the inside of this tower or any presidential tower again."

"You don't believe that or else you wouldn't have called me here."

"You don't have the strength to be president," she shouted. "You are causing chaos!"

"Causing chaos? What do you think has been happening for the last twenty years?" I cried.

"We have been a successfully growing nation ever since I took office."

"We have been through war, and we have been suffering ever since."

"War?" she spat. "You don't *know* suffering."

"I've lived through the overpopulation, the war, and now this. I've known plenty of suffering."

"The gas solved the overpopulation problem," she stated unequivocally.

"Solved it? What about all the people who were killed and the ones who weren't ... the Sleepers?"

"We didn't plan for the Sleepers ... they were an unfortunate and unseen side effect of the gas. It didn't make itself present in the animal testing."

"You *knew* about the gas?" I shuddered.

"Foolish girl. *We* released the gas. Population control, specifically a *certain* population, is part of governmental responsibility. The Elites were warned of the incoming attack ahead of time, of course."

Rage built inside of me with each word she spoke.

"All the people you killed ... my mother!" I yelled. "You're a murderer!"

I leaped up and stormed out of the meeting. My heart pounded and my eyes filled with tears. I thought about my mother as sadness and anger fought to be my prevailing emotion.

Torrent killed her. Torrent killed them all!

I had to run far away from Torrent and this tower fast. Now that I knew the truth about the gas attack, she would surely try to kill me to keep her tactics concealed. Speeding down the hall toward the elevator, I noticed four men following me. I glanced around and saw four more men down by the elevator. I made a quick turn and pushed open the stairwell instead. Bolting down the steps quickly, I reached the bottom floor. I pushed open the stairwell door, which led me to a dark hallway.

There was a door that read, "EXIT." I pushed it, but it was locked. I tried the other doors. The sound of footsteps was getting closer.

Then, the door that was marked "EXIT" flung open. I didn't have time to wonder how it had opened.

I ran out of the building.

The door had led to a wide alleyway, and each turn I took brought me to a new alley, all of which were cluttered by the broken glass and debris that littered the rest of the world. The large mounds of garbage were the only things protecting me. I heard two gunshots behind me, but I guessed that the Mules couldn't get a lock on me because I was still running. I tried to keep my head down as I sped fast down the path and around the corners, but I couldn't see an end to this. I couldn't outrun the men chasing me, and they knew these backstreets better than I did. When I looked back last, there were five of them on my tail. I turned back again, but I only saw three this time. I rounded another corner and continued to run but stopped dead in my tracks.

A dead end.

No!

The brick wall extended three stories high on all sides of me. There was a ladder on the wall in front of me. It looked like an old fire escape, but I wouldn't have been able to climb it before they rounded the corner. There was a door to the left.

I tried to open it feverishly, but it was locked.

I felt my heart beating in my ears. I spun around quickly and saw the three men in uniform lined up blocking my only way out. I knew for sure that they were going to kill me.

I braced for the gunfire, but they didn't shoot.

Their orders must have been to take me in alive. They were going to make me their Puppet. I thought about what would happen to everyone else.

Dad.

Theo.

Lou.

I couldn't think about them now. I kicked off my shoes.

Climb!

As I climbed frantically, I saw a figure appear at the top of the ladder. I froze in fear as the sun glared in my eyes. I couldn't make out who it was at first. If it was another one of Torrent's Mules, I could consider myself a goner. I squinted as I stared up at the figure allowing my eyes to adjust to the light. The sun shined down through fiery red locks of hair.

"I've got you covered. Come on up, El," It was Conan, the leader of the Hunters. I rushed anxiously up to him.

"Get lost, Hoodlum! We have orders to take her in alive but you on the other hand—" a Secret Service agent hollered up to him.

"I don't think so," Conan replied. "What, you thought she didn't have protection?"

I braced myself for the gunfire.

"I wouldn't even think about it," said Theo. He was directly behind one of the Secret Service agents, with a gun to his head.

I looked up and saw thirty or forty of the BK12 and the upstate Hunters perched on the rooftops and down below in the alleys.

"Is this really a fight you want to get involved with?" the Secret Serviceman asked. "Get lost!"

"That's my sister," Theo replied proudly, before pulling the trigger and shooting the man in the head. There was nothing my brother wouldn't do to protect me.

I saw Sanzhar, Theo's friend from the BK12, shoot another guard, and one of the Hunters shot the third with his crossbow. The Secret Serviceman's walkie-talkie went off with a beep. It was Torrent's voice coming from the other side.

"Agent Smith, has it been handled?" There were only a few seconds before there was another beep.

"Agent Smith?"

Theo picked the walkie up off of the ground. "I'm sorry, Agent Smith can't come to the phone right now," he said.

Without letting go of the receiver, Theo pointed his gun back at Smith's head and pulled the trigger. I imagined that the gunshot echoed on the other end of the line.

I hurried across the roof and down the other side of the building to the main street, where a car was waiting for me. One of the Hunters was driving. Sanzhar, Theo, and Conan stayed behind to handle the Secret Service. The sound of gunshots and screams were all I heard as I ducked into the car and sped away.

Chapter Twelve

I knew then more than ever that we needed to win. I couldn't accuse Torrent's administration of releasing the gas without proof or I would be considered a conspiracy theorist, which would turn the people against me. The people of Brooklyn and the surrounding area knew who I was. Some communities around the suburbs and countryside had even heard of our movement. Out west there were groups of people who knew my name, too. But that wasn't going to be enough.

By next week the entire nation would know my name because our first and only debate was scheduled for next Tuesday. The problem was that the One Network aired the debate, and it was under government control. Pratt had said that my words would be cut and edited. There was no way to tell the public that the questions would be unfair and, of course, skewed in Torrent's favor.

There was one radio station dedicated to our cause that operated out of a remote cabin up in the Adirondack Mountains. I needed to go there, and after I told Pratt about what had happened with the police officers on the Brooklyn Bridge the other day, he vowed to never let me go anywhere unprotected again.

I stood in the apartment staring at my luggage, a shirt, two pairs of socks, and some underwear stuffed into a small *I Love NY* backpack. I looked like I was about to hitchhike cross-country.

"You travel light for a girl," Pratt said, glancing at my luggage. We were going to be gone for two to three days at most, so one change of clothes was plenty. "Are you ready?"

"Yeah, I think so," I lied. Pratt saw through it.

"What's wrong? Are you missing your toothbrush or something?" he joked.

"Yeah, that and my sanity," I laughed back. I didn't want to burden Pratt with my problems and more than that, I wasn't sure if he was the right person to vent to. But for some reason at that moment, it felt easy.

"I'm not special," I said. "This revolution ... this movement ... it isn't mine. I barely know basic algebra yet somehow; I am competing to run a nation? I'm a fraud." I winced at my own words. Saying it out loud sounded harsher than it did in my head.

Pratt took a moment to process my words, and then he took a slow step forward. "I see." He looked at the pictures of my family on the walls. He spotted one of me with Lou and Theo taken back before the gas attack.

He pointed at Lou. "There's my girl." He smiled and then looked back at me. "Does she think you're a fraud?" I took a deep breath preparing to defend myself, but he continued. "And your brother, does he think you're a fraud?"

I started to speak, but he interrupted me again.

"Well? These are the people who know you best. Tell me why is it they believe in you?"

"That's the thing. I don't know why."

"I wonder if it because you don't see yourself clearly. Maybe you have put other people first your entire life, and now you don't know how to believe in yourself." He walked steadily closer to me with each word. "People believe in you because you're strong. You're loyal. You keep your word. You go out of your way to help others. You light up a room with your smile, and you inspire others to become better versions of themselves."

He was only inches away from me. My stomach was in a knot, and I wasn't sure if it was due to my nerves for this trip or the way he was looking at me.

"I don't even know what I'm doing half the time. I'm just a nobody from nowhere, and all these people think I'm this leader with all the answers. I don't have the answers. It's very possible I am the wrong person for this job ... and maybe I'm a bad person for making these people believe in me when I don't even believe in myself."

Pratt was staring straight into my eyes.

"I've been hired to do many terrible things," he said, not breaking eye contact for even a second. "Things that weren't right. This isn't one of them. This is a good thing, and *you* are the right person."

He took a breath before continuing. "You don't have to have all the answers. Your honesty in knowing that you don't have all the answers might be the best thing about you ... my favorite thing about you. That, and your smile."

I smiled.

He smiled back. "There it is ..."

I put my backpack in the backseat and hopped into the passenger side of Pratt's truck. It was a five-hour drive to get upstate to the Adirondacks where the radio headquarters was. Not too many people knew its exact location. We had been invited to come speak on air by messenger.

It had been a cold September, and it was supposed to be dropping down to the forties at night, that much we prepared for. I had my coat, hat, and gloves all packed. What we weren't prepared for, however, was the rain. It was one in the afternoon when the storm rolled in. Pratt drove for a while as buckets of water poured down the windshield. The only thing lighting the roads was the occasional flash of lightning. We contemplated pulling over under a bridge to wait out the storm, but the cold night was approaching.

"Albany," I read, barely making out the sign through the rain. "We can stop at my grandmother's house." I had been there once before when we went to help Nan move after my aunt passed away.

Pratt turned off the exit. Once inside we lit a fire and ate some of the food we had packed. It was a comfortable home. It hadn't been lived in for eight years, which was evident by the bugs, dust, and occasional sign of rodents. We shook out a few of Nan's old wool blankets and sat close to the fireplace. Even with the fire roaring it was freezing cold. Pratt took a bottle out of his bag and took a sip.

"What is that?" I asked.

"It's something to warm me up." He looked at me warily and then handed me the bottle.

"Oh, no thanks."

We talked about the Laissez-Faire and Brooklyn while we ate our meal and waited for the storm to pass. When it didn't, we figured we might have to stay the night. We discussed finding a house with electricity, but Pratt said the storm was too severe and that we should stay put. He went to find some pillows, and when he came back, he found me shivering even more so than before.

"Maybe I'll take you up on that drink," I said, looking up at him. He gave me the bottle, and I took a swig. It was absolutely disgusting, but I felt warmer. I took another swig.

We laid close to the fire with one blanket under us and one over us. Pratt's body heat was radiating under the covers. But since we didn't have any more firewood, and the wood outside would be too wet to burn, I knew I would be cold again when the last of the fire burned out. However, for the moment, the liquor had proven effective in both keeping me warm and making me extra talkative.

"I'm sorry about all of this," I sighed.

"You're sorry that your grandmother hasn't paid an electric bill in a house she hasn't lived in for eight years? Or are you sorry about the weather?" Pratt asked sarcastically.

"You wouldn't be here if it weren't for me. I should have come alone."

"And driven what? Do you even have a license?"

"You'd let me borrow your car." I smiled.

"Try to get some sleep. You have a big day tomorrow."

I closed my eyes, and then popped them open and propped myself up on my elbow. "Pratt?" I whispered. Whatever was in the bottle had worked its way straight to my head.

"Yes."

"How old are you?"

"Twenty-five."

"Why don't you have a girlfriend or a wife?" I asked with genuine curiosity.

"I've never looked for one," Pratt responded earnestly.

"I hope I have someone by the time I'm twenty-five," I said, as I laid my head back on my pillow.

"You have Kai."

"Kai? No, we are just friends," I explained.

"Does *he* know that?" Pratt scoffed.

"He doesn't even like me like that."

"Everyone that meets you likes you like that."

"No!" I shrieked, appalled that he thought that. It surely wasn't true. "What about you? All the girls like you." I turned the accusation on him, and it was the truth.

"Oh, really. '*All* the girls?'" Pratt mocked.

"Gianna thinks you're hot." I could tell she did by the way she looked at him.

"I'm not interested in Gianna."

"Well, what is it you're looking for?"

"I'm looking to get some sleep," Pratt said, as he turned his head away from me.

"Imagine if we were just some twenty-one and twenty-five-year-olds in another time," I said. "Back in the 1990s or something. And this was our house," I smiled at the thought.

"We are two people huddled together under one blanket next to a dying fire. We would be called destitute by their standards."

"I mean, what if we had jobs. You were in the military, and I was a nurse, and we came home at night and ate dinner in the kitchen, and talked about our day. Then we went to sleep in the bedroom and talked about our dreams before falling asleep." I looked over at Pratt. "What are your dreams?"

"I don't have dreams anymore."

"Why not?"

"Some people don't deserve dreams."

"Everyone deserves a dream."

"Not me."

"Why?"

"We should get some sleep."

"Tell me," I demanded.

"El, you're drunk."

"So, that's even more reason to tell me. I won't remember it in the morning anyway."

"I've killed people," he said.

"You were a soldier. It was your job."

"No. I killed Americans."

"Oh," I hesitated. "Why?"

"Because I was ordered to," Pratt replied. "I followed orders blindly, and I went against my beliefs."

"But you've changed. You're not that person anymore."

"The fact that I've changed won't bring back the people I've killed," he said. "You asked about my father and brother. The U.S. government killed them because of me. When I enlisted in the army, I signed a waiver signing my life over to the military. I was a good fighter ... 'the best,' they said. I worked my way up the ranks quickly.

"After I was ordered to kill Americans and refused, I tried to leave. But Torrent wouldn't allow it. Blindly following Torrent's orders was in the paperwork. But I couldn't kill men who did nothing but disagree with the tyrant.

"The Forces came looking for me but found one of our militia bases instead. My father, my brother, and his wife and their daughter, along with my team were there. They killed them all. I went to kill Torrent myself, but she told me she still had my niece alive and living in an Elite Village with a new family. She said that if I wanted her to stay safe, I would continue my work with the military until my term was up." He took a deep breath.

"What's her name?" I asked.

"Abigail."

"Did you get to see her?" I asked.

"No. That was part of the deal. I had to stay away. I don't know if it was the right choice, but I had to do it for my brother's sake."

"If we don't win, we will get her. We can take her, Lou, and everyone else away from the city or we can live in the Bedrock."

"We're *going* to win."

Pratt's phone rang. He listened to a voice on the other end, and then he said that we had to move.

"There's a storm out there. Can't we just sleep?" I slurred, still lying down. The alcohol had proved to be too much for me. I didn't think I could keep my eyes open a minute longer. Pratt scooped me up, carrying me to the truck. I fell asleep while he drove.

I couldn't say how long I was asleep, but when I woke up, it felt as though I had been asleep for days. I was in an unfamiliar bed in an unfamiliar room. The bed had a canopy with silk panels covering all four sides. I pulled aside one of the curtains to look around. It was a grand room. There was a chandelier in the center of a pitched ceiling, and stuffed upholstered chairs and chaise lounges accented the floor length windows. There were scattered rugs throughout the room. I put a foot to the ground. The wooden floors were cold, so I quickly moved my foot onto a bearskin rug instead. I ran my toes against the velvety fur.

It wasn't until I had passed a mirror that I noticed what I was wearing. I was wearing woman's pajamas, a white silk top, and matching pants all under the softest white cotton robe. I quickly pulled down my pants to see what underpants I had on. They were the same ones. *Thank God.* I was embarrassed at the thought of Pratt changing my clothes. I guessed he had forgotten to grab our luggage before we bolted out of Nan's cottage. I strolled out of the room and toward the sound of clanking plates and silverware in the kitchen.

"Good morning, Sunshine," Pratt chirped when he saw me round the corner.

The kitchen seemed to be the focal point of the house, almost like a hub with other rooms and hallways extending from it. The granite countertop lined the entire circumference of the room, breaking only for the entryways into the other rooms. There was a large island of solid wood and granite in the middle of the kitchen with extravagant light fixtures hanging above it. Eight tall bar stools were set around it. I pulled out one of the stools and sat down. Pratt's hands were in the sink. He turned to me and smiled, and I gestured down at my clothes. His smile faded.

"Oh, right," he said, looking at the soapy water in front of him. "Your clothes were wet, and you were asleep. I didn't want you to get sick." He turned toward me. "I didn't change your—"

"I know," I said quickly. "Thanks."

A smile came back on his face. I've met creeps in my life, and he wasn't one of them. I knew his intentions to keep me dry were innocent.

"How'd you sleep?" he asked.

"Really good, actually," I responded. I hadn't felt that refreshed for as far back as I could remember.

Pratt brought a plate over and placed it down in front of me—blueberry waffles and maple syrup. "Do you drink coffee with milk?" he asked, spinning around and grabbing a fork and knife from the drawer.

I nodded and picked up the fork at the same time. I hadn't thought I was hungry, but the smell of syrup set my stomach rumbling. I took a bite, and Pratt put a cup of coffee in front of me. He went to the cupboard and grabbed a can of milk. He opened it and poured some into my cup. The coffee lightened as I watched the white milk form lines and shapes.

"Sugar?" he asked.

"Yes, please," I replied.

While he went back to the cupboard, I analyzed the room. The ceilings must have been twenty feet high with exposed beams. It smelled like cedar and crisp linen. The cedar scent was from the wood and the linen scent, I assumed, was from the upholstered stools and benches. The room itself had an industrial feel yet there were feminine touches like white throw pillows on the breakfast nook by the kitchen pantry. I had never seen pillows in a kitchen before.

My eyes stopped on a portrait above the stone fireplace. It was of a beautiful young woman with golden hair curled down past her shoulders. Her skin was fair, and her lips were painted dark red. Pratt must have seen me staring at the girl.

"That's Ermelinda," he said.

"Oh?" I said, trying not to sound too interested.

"I was her bodyguard." He walked back over to the sink and pulled a dish out of the water. "She had this house custom built for herself six years ago, and she's been here maybe five times at most. She has other houses in California, the Hamptons, and Phoenix. I don't think she's even been to New York this year."

"She's beautiful, you must miss her." I wasn't a fool. I could tell by the way he was talking about her that they had had a relationship.

"Yes, she's beautiful. And no, I don't miss her," Pratt said, drying his hands with a dishtowel. He was looking up at her portrait.

"Why not?"

"I don't know. You can't tell why you miss someone. You just do, or you don't."

He said the radio headquarters was only two hours away. Two hours wasn't a long trip, but I felt filthy from the night and sitting in the car for that long would only make it worse. I didn't want to admit it, but part of me wished he had changed my underpants.

"Is there a bathroom where I can freshen up before we leave?"

"Go to the top floor. It's the last door at the end of the hallway," he directed. "And take your time. I have some things I want to get done around here."

I had never been inside such a lavish home. I felt out of place. It seemed like the walls themselves would realize I didn't belong and kick me out. I felt like I was inside a movie set. The high ceilings had windows on them in certain spots, so that you could see the sky right above you. It allowed the sunlight to shine through, lighting the white walls in an iridescent glow. The wooden floors under my feet were accented with scattered rugs of fur and wool. The stairwell was the grandest part of all. It was wide, and as it ascended, it diverged into two directions. "The left wing," I remembered Pratt saying. I headed off to the left.

There were framed images of nature and people, but most were of this woman herself, which I found peculiar. One photo that caught my eye was of a Division that looked a lot like ours. The photo was of a long line at a Rations Center that wrapped around the building. Adults and children gathered, waiting for their monthly rations. I read the caption below: Chicago 2027. I shook my head.

Only an Elite could find beauty in such an image. I walked up the stairs and down the hall to the last door like Pratt said.

"Whoa," I gasped as I walked into the room. The large dome-shaped room was covered almost entirely from floor to ceiling with large beige tiles that were accented with glistening dark tan smaller squares. The cathedral ceiling was made entirely of glass, illuminating the room. The sunbeams shot down and warmed my face, as I stared up at the sky above. A white claw foot tub sat majestically in the center of the room. I walked over it and turned the cold water on first, and then the hot. Steam came rising from the bath.

I was surprised by how excited I was to bathe. The last bath I had was in the sink when I was a baby. I showered twice a week at home, but water had been capped in the cities since I was ten-years-old. The government claimed it was part of the Green Peace Deal to preserve water. However, the Elites water supply wasn't capped. Many Elites had swimming pools and watered their lawns. Each Division was allocated only so much, and by the end of the month, we typically ran out of running water. A quick shower twice a week was what I was used to. I could see how the Elites, or anyone for that matter, could get used to this.

A large freestanding mirror stood to the right alongside a cedar cabinet. White towels were folded neatly on the bottom shelf of the cabinet. I walked over and unfolded one. The plush fabric was unlike any I had ever felt before. I rubbed it against my cheek and then stuck my face in it entirely. It smelled like roses.

I looked at myself in the mirror while I undressed. I didn't look like that woman in the pictures around the house. My hair was stringy, and unlike her voluminous figure and fair skin, my body was thin and tan from the sun. I combed my hair with my fingers trying to give it a little volume. I stuck my butt out and pursed my lips together while giving my reflection my best puppy dog eyes. I guess I looked a little bit more like her when I did that. I laughed to myself. I placed my towel over the side of the tub and stepped into it slowly.

The water was hot, and it engulfed me swiftly. I lay back and took a deep breath. I read the labels on the bubble baths, which were lined up on the side of the tub: rose, lavender, and chamomile. I uncapped the rose and poured some in. Bubbles quickly filled the tub and spilled down to the floor.

"Oops!" I gasped. I guessed it was okay to make a little mess. From what Pratt said this woman wouldn't be at this house anytime soon. I had seen bubble baths on the vid before, but I had never had one. I scooped up a handful of bubbles and blew them away. They smelled heavenly. I breathed them in, and I leaned back to look up at the sky. Then I closed my eyes and drifted away. I allowed my body and mind to be taken over by the warm water and scent. *I could see why the Elites didn't want to give this up.* Who wouldn't want this life? A bath was a simple pleasure, but it was one that even a Hoodlum should be allowed to enjoy occasionally.

Suddenly I heard a loud crash. I sat up quickly, splashing a good amount of water out of the tub. I sat still and looked around. No more than ten seconds later Pratt came running in.

"El!" he yelled. He looked at me and turned around quickly. "Sorry. I heard something."

"I heard it, too," I said. Pratt was wearing a black fitted T-shirt and blue jeans that fit him just right, with black boots, while I was naked. It seemed unfair. I slid down further into the water.

"I'll go check it out. Could be a downed tree with this wind." He turned halfway to me, not making eye contact.

"You're okay though?" he asked.

I took in the way he looked in those jeans, his perfect hair, and his rugged voice, and I realized I didn't want him to leave. I wanted him to turn back around to me.

"I'm okay," I assured him. "I bet it was a tree." I sat up slightly, exposing my bare shoulders. He looked at me. I felt his eyes on my skin, and my heart began to beat excessively. I stopped breathing for a moment.

He swallowed hard, and his words came out broken at first. "I should go check it out." He motioned toward the door.

I stared back at him, still holding my breath.

He turned to walk out of the room. Then he turned around again. "You look really nice in bubbles."

As he walked out of the room, the air that I had been holding captive in my lungs escaped feverishly in the form of popping bubbles as I sunk down under the water. He made my heart beat out of my chest. I needed to get out of the bathtub before I became overheated.

I hurried out of the tub and dressed into one of Ermelinda's relaxed denim jeans and a red top that lay limp on my thin body. I imagined that her curves filled out the shirt much better. By the time I scurried downstairs, Pratt already had the truck started and was loading up some water bottles and food.

"You ready?" He opened the door for me.

I wasn't ready to leave the comforts of this palace. Even one more night's sleep in that bed would leave me rested for life, but I nodded and climbed back into the truck. There was work to do.

We headed off toward the radio headquarters. Pratt sang along to his angry music.

"You're an awful singer you know that?" I said, laughing.

He sang louder and even more off tune just to spite me, I was sure. I covered my ears, but secretly I listened to each word and followed each note as off-key as they were. His music was similar to the music Dad used to listen to when I was a kid. 'Rock and Roll' I believed they called it. The only music I ever heard on the vid or radio was highly censored pop that was about one of three things: love, lost love, or lust. It grew old fast. This angst-filled music Pratt sang was intriguing.

A couple of hours later, we pulled off the side road we had been driving on to an even smaller and windier road. The truck bounced along the rock and gravel.

"How much further?" I asked. I was eager to get to the radio station for two reasons. One, I was eager to tell the nation about our agenda. Two, I was about to be carsick. We came to the end of the road.

"Where is it?" I asked anxiously.

"It's here," Pratt announced confidently. I looked around. Maybe I was missing something because I didn't see anything but mountains and trees.

He turned off the truck and started walking. I followed right behind him. Beyond some straggly pines and between two large boulders there it was—the cabin. It was set so high in the mountain and hidden so deep in the pines that the Elites could never find it. The large satellite was camouflaged by a rock of the same color. The front door was open and inside was a man and his dog—Worley Jones and Tonto. I knew their names from listening to the radio show.

"Welcome, welcome!" the man hollered from behind a coffee mug. He took a big swig of whatever liquid was in the cup, and then he extended his arms out to his sides extravagantly.

"Welcome!" he repeated, sending the remains of whatever was in his cup flying out. His eyes were wild, and his grin exposed yellowed teeth. The golden wheaten terrier that ran circles around Worley's feet went to lick up what was flung.

Worley's station was the one and only non-Elite radio signal, which is why he was hidden in the mountains. His radio's signal had been able to dodge the Elites' attempts to take it down. He broadcasted on a guerilla network that the Elites couldn't permeate.

We went inside and looked around. The cabin was one large room. I think there was a toilet in the closet. I didn't care to take a closer look. His equipment was old, but that is what gave him an edge. His portals were obsolete by modern standards, so they were undetectable by the Elites' surveillance software.

"Well, how about the Grand Tour?" Worley asked, enthusiastically.

He bustled about frantically, from one wall to another pointing out the framed photos of the celebrities and politicians he had met, along with newspaper clippings about himself while Pratt and I followed him cautiously around the small cabin.

"One thing is for certain ... you can't beat this view," he said, pulling back an old tapestry he had hanging on the wall to reveal a large window that overlooked the entire mountain range. As far as the eye could see were snowcapped mountains and untouched nature.

"Yeah, Tonto and I have the life up here. Don't get me wrong, though, we love having visitors. Come sit down." He gestured for me to sit in an old wooden chair across from his station. It had a lumpy and torn red pillow on top of it, for cushioning, I guessed.

"You ready to speak to the country?" he asked, making his way over to his seat behind the microphone. "They've been waiting for this for a long time now."

I was nervous, but I gave no hint to it. I wanted to live up to what everyone thought I was. What I *wanted* to be.

"Oh, I'm so rude," Worley interjected. "What would you like to drink? We have water, coffee ... what else do we have, Tonto?"

Tonto barked.

"Oh, yes. We have some whiskey," he bubbled, lifting his mug up with a grin.

"I'm fine, thank you," I said politely as I sat down in my chair at the other microphone. Tonto jumped into my lap and positioned himself for a nap. I shifted on the pillow and settled into place.

"I'm ready," I said confidently enough to even fool myself. And so, the interview ensued. I clearly spoke the truth about the movement, the government, and the Elites. I detailed all that we had done so far, and all that we had planned to do. When asked of the Elites and their deception, I was careful not to say too much about their involvement in the gas attack. If I did, I would sound like a conspiracy theorist, and that would only turn voters off. We already had con artists and hacks in the political realm; accusations without proof weren't what the people wanted to hear. So, I talked about the facts; the violence in the streets, the lack of education, the lack of jobs, and the dependence on the government. Then it was over, the one chance we had to communicate with the entire nation directly, unedited, and unfiltered by the media bias.

We sent out our message, and we headed home. We waved goodbye to Worley and Tonto, leaving them with the food we had taken from Ermelinda's house. The night was clear, and we drove straight through it, arriving home to Brooklyn in the early hours of the following morning.

Chapter Thirteen

Debate Night

The day had passed so quickly as did the days before. I couldn't believe the night was finally here. Kai and I stayed up until two in the morning practicing my answers and refining my onstage presence. He told me that I tended to scowl when I was nervous, so I'd have to keep that in mind throughout the debate because nothing was scarier than a smiling mouth with scowling eyes.

    I peered out into the audience from backstage. The venue was packed, it was a large old theatre outside of Manhattan. The center stage was illuminated with lights that hung from the ceiling, and additional spotlights were set up on both sides of the stage. The entire scene was mesmerizing, really. There were three cameramen on crane-like devices positioned in front of the stage. They practiced moving their equipment around as the crowd settled into their seats. The moderator hadn't taken his seat yet, but I saw his box seat high above center stage and pushed back behind the podiums. I was standing there with Kai, Theo, and Lonnie.

    "I feel ridiculous," Lonnie mumbled. She was in full disguise. We had managed to find a few items from Dad, Mr. Maxwell, and Pratt, which made for an interesting combination. The Elites, and especially some government officials would easily be able to recognize her as Mr. Berea's daughter if it weren't for one of Dad's trench coats, a pair of Pratt's old wind goggles, and Mr. Maxwell's worn leather cowboy hat.

"You look fine," I said. I had to hide a chuckle. She really did look ridiculous. The amusement came as a relief to me as I was beginning to get the sweats thinking about the announcer calling me to stage. I guess my nerves began to show.

"You got this," Kai assured me. "We've practiced every possible question a million and ten times."

I knew he was right. I had practiced every question and rehearsed every answer. I knew my opponent's weakness, and I had my notecards. I wasn't prepared, however, for it to be one hundred degrees on stage. The debate was to be broadcasted live on the One Network, and the ividcam broadcasted nationwide, which meant my face was going to be on every block in every Division for all Americans to see. I felt like I was going to be sick. At that moment I knew I needed to eat something or I'd pass out.

"Candidates to the stage," a production assistant shouted.

Kai and Lonnie both turned to me excitedly and I forced a smile. I felt my eyes go into a deep scowl.

"Uhh ..." Kai said, scratching the back of his neck and turning away slightly.

"You're doing it again, creepy," Lonnie cringed.

I closed my eyes, took a deep breath and then exhaled loudly. I thought about roses, the smell of tomatoes on the vine, and Tonto napping on his little red pillow, and then I opened my eyes and smiled. Kai nodded his head and returned the smile.

"Perfect," he said.

"Okay guys, this is it. Wish me luck." I sounded much more casual than I had intended. We all knew what was riding on this debate. Lonnie's foot was tapping loudly, and Kai couldn't stop fidgeting with the pencil in his hand. I wasn't sure who was more nervous, them or me. Kai leaned in and embraced me tightly. His hug was a warm bed on a cold night. The pressure of his body eased my tension.

"You got this," he whispered in my ear. As he pulled away, I grabbed his hand and squeezed it tightly. He had always been a security blanket for me. Tonight, more than ever, I was thankful to have him here with me.

Lonnie pushed through and gave me a big squeeze. "Get 'em, girl!" she said, kissing my cheek. "It's all about confidence."

I had to hold back a chuckle again as I looked at her goggles and trench coat. I took a deep breath and stepped out from behind the curtain. The bright lights only became more blinding as I walked deeper onto the stage. I squinted as I made my way toward the far-left podium, while smiling, of course. The camera was not yet turned on, but the crowd had settled in and was looking on intently. I glanced at Torrent's empty podium. I could hear polite applause and even a few cheers from the crowd along with some louder jeers as I set my notecards up on the podium in front of me and adjusted the microphone to my height.

Suddenly, the applause echoed louder, and the lights seemed to shine brighter as well. The curtain had drawn back from center stage to reveal Torrent. Supporters in the crowd leaped out of their seats in wild ovation. It was as though a rock star was stepping on stage.

Torrent was wearing a full white pantsuit with comically large red buttons, I don't think they were even functional buttons, rather show buttons. Her broad smile looked painted on, and her teeth were as white as the lights that, by now, I was sure had permanently blinded me. Her black hair was perfectly curled under her chin, and her nails were freshly manicured a bright shade of red, as she waved to the audience while taking her position behind the podium. She looked somehow fake, like a character in a cartoon. I wouldn't have been surprised if she broke out into a dance right there on the stage in front of me, but she didn't. She stood behind her podium, smiling and mock talking to "friends" in the front row although I was certain that she, just like me, couldn't see a foot in front of her face. As I adjusted my notecards once more, I noticed that she didn't have any. I had been watching her, but she didn't look at me once. I turned my head straight and took another deep breath. I saw the lights from the cameras turn from red to green. The camera cranes began to dance their rehearsed dips and spins.

The debate had begun.

"Welcome to Debate Night 2046. Tonight, we are in for a treat with the first debate we've had since 2024," the moderator called from high above the stage.

I tried to look at anything other than the lights, but there was little else to see. I did my best to keep an even posture and a smile on my face. Despite all of my rallies and every hour upon hour of practice, this was something completely daunting to me. The moderator sat high above the stage behind us. I couldn't see him, but I knew he was there.

"We welcome to the stage this evening our two candidates for President of the United States of America ... presidential hopeful Elisha Logan, and the current President of the United States, Lorrent Torrent."

I saw Torrent wince at the announcement and tightly grab the corners of her podium, but her perfectly adjusted smile didn't waver. I don't believe I had ever heard her first name before. I had always assumed it was just Torrent, kind of like OZ.

The debate questions started out forthright.

"Ms. Logan, can you tell us about your plan to eliminate the Rations Centers?" he asked.

"I believe the Rations Centers are used as a crutch in our society. While we get enough to eat to keep us alive, we get nothing more. I wouldn't eliminate the

Rations Centers immediately ... we need them to get us on our feet. But we can open the gate to local grocery shops and restaurants that will boost the economy and soon there will be little need for government food programs."

"President Torrent, how do you feel about that?" he asked.

"Well, when you view the world through a child's eyes it may seem that simple, but where are the people going to earn enough money to shop at these local stores and eat at these local restaurants? Food is a right to all people, not an earned reward."

The crowd erupted in cheers.

"President Torrent," the moderator began, "how do you sleep at night knowing how many people you've killed? The moderator adjusted his notecards. "Wait ... what is this?" There was an awkward shuffle in the crowd.

Torrent's perfect smile faded briefly.

"I'm sorry, I seemed to have gotten my questions mixed up," he stammered. "President Torrent, how many of the Divisions do you visit on a regular basis?"

"I visit each one at least once a month via ividcam. I like to check in and connect, not just with the people in the Northeast, but with the people everywhere. It would be inconsiderate to only visit the people in one region."

I knew where this was going.

"And Ms. Logan," the moderator sneered, "how many Divisions have you visited in the past year while you've been campaigning?"

"I don't have access to hologram travel," I said. "But I've visited every Division in Brooklyn, and many in New York, Philadelphia, and parts of New Jersey."

"So only the people in the Northeast matter to you?"

"Of course not," I responded. "Like I said, I don't have access to hologram travel so journeying to other regions is difficult."

"Yes, when things become difficult, certain people just give up," the moderator sighed.

The questions only seemed to become stranger. Torrent was asked about her accomplishments and policy plan, while I was asked about my parents and Theo. I tried to switch the talking points to policy, but the moderator continued directing the conversation back to nonsense.

"Your brother, Theodore, is part of the BK12 gang. Can you tell us, have you ever committed a crime with him?"

I turned around and looked up at the debate monitor. He was sitting with a large book in front of him. He peered around it and looked down at me.

"Are you going to answer the question?" I felt the camera close in on my face.

"No, I have never committed a crime," I spoke directly to the moderator.

"So, you're saying you didn't steal with him?" he queried again.

I thought back to the time Theo stole deli cookies when I was eleven. *Can he seriously be talking about that?*

"He, I mean *we*, took cookies from a store when we were kids, but—" I didn't even finish my sentence. The jeers from the audience boomed.

Torrent nodded, "Calm down everyone." She raised her hands palms forward, and then lowered them. "Now, she was a kid. Let's not judge her too harshly; we all make mistakes when we are kids. In fact, she is *still* a kid ... not suitable for office. Why she doesn't even know her ABCs!" Torrent snickered, and a large group cackle echoed from the audience, too.

"I'm not a child," I interrupted vehemently.

"And like a child she is selfish. She is trying to take away your health insurance, your food, and your housing. And to that, I say, NO. NO, little girl!"

The audience broke into a loud cheer. I felt like I was already losing grip so early on in the debate. *I prepared for all of this, how they would twist my words, ask unfair questions, and mock my age.* I knew I couldn't argue with her or return her insults, doing so would only make me look like the child she was claiming me to be. I needed to get to the point and fast, and this was my one shot to do it. I thought about Dad, Lou, and my mom. I had to do it for them, for us all.

"You're right, Torrent," I said, as I looked up from my notecards. "I do want to take those things away. We, the people, don't want the things you offer. We are taking away the net above our heads ... the net that was put there and is held in place by your administration's abomination of democracy. Now we can rise.

"You think handing us some food and clothing for our monthly rations will keep us blind to your misdeeds? You think allowing us to live in the ghetto for sliding scale rent will keep us quiet? Do you think keeping our foods unhealthy and our schools in shambles will keep our children from excelling? The only time I saw you care was when our drug problem moved into your Villages. Did you really think no one would ever catch on?

"Where is your net, Mrs. Torrent? You will soon feel it. You are starting to feel it now, aren't you? Do you feel it closing in on you? We have you right where we want you, and we aren't under your control anymore. It's our time! There will be no division between the Elites and as the government calls us, *Hoodlums*. We will be one people.

"There is a reason why the Tower has no wall ... it isn't needed. The walls were never meant to keep the Hoodlums out of the Elite Village; it was meant to keep us separated. Because when we are divided, we are weak, but together we are strong. Our food will not be tainted with chemicals, our schools will have good teachers, our husbands and wives will have jobs in high-rise towers, and we will be able to open our own businesses and have free trade. We will have a standard of quality for all Americans, not just for the Elites. Safe homes and quality education aren't a luxury meant just for the few. Our souls are not yours for the keeping, Mrs. Torrent. Not anymore."

The crowd was silent. I swallowed hard and stood up straight. I felt the lights shining hot on my face. I heard a small clap, followed by another. Pretty soon there were some whistles and cheers. I smiled. If my words reached some of the people in this audience, then maybe, just maybe, they reached some of the millions of people watching at home.

Kai and Lonnie rushed to greet me as I exited the stage.

"You did great!" Kai exclaimed. He could barely stand still.

"That was amazing," Lonnie added, dancing around. Her wide eyes and light feet matched how I felt.

Torrent plowed through the curtains backstage. Bruna, Torrent's loyal assistant, was there waiting for her.

"Why did they use my first name, you know I hate my first name!" Torrent screamed.

We saw Bruna scramble for an answer as Torrent marched away with Bruna trailing right behind her.

Lonnie and Kai laughed.

"Wait, so her name is Lorrent Torrent?" I asked.

"Yeah," Lonnie chortled. "Kai and I hacked into the moderator's notes. We tried to adjust the questions too, but it looks like he caught on."

It was fine. Even with the unfair questions, I had conveyed my point in the end. And seeing Torrent that angry put a smile on all of our faces.

Chapter Fourteen

The moderator was an asshole. But he was right about one thing, the election was at the national level, not just state. We had spent time rallying in New York, Pennsylvania, and New Jersey, but we had to meet with the citizens out West. I had never left the comforts of the Northeast, but if I were to be President, I would be President to *all* the people. How could I govern states I had never even seen? I was going to head out West and meet the people.

Kai, Lonnie, Pratt, and Lee offered to come with me. I told them that the fewer people who knew about the trip, the better. Torrent and her Mules would like nothing more than to know I was in the middle of the desert at the mercy of the Elites' highway patrolmen. We decided it was safer to go with just the five of us because bringing the security team would cause too much of a scene. Theo lent us motorbikes from the BK12. I drove with Kai, Lonnie rode with Lee, and Pratt rode alone.

"These things operate on solar power. You're good to go as long as it doesn't rain," Theo had said.

We had mapped out a route to Arizona, looping around to Montana, and heading back toward Indiana, and then home. We estimated we would be gone for sixteen days. The ride out through the desert was long, and there wasn't much to see. The land west of Pennsylvania had fallen to wasteland a long time ago when private companies were banned. With no Rations

Centers nearby and no grocery stores, those one-horse fly over states just didn't survive.

Our first glimpse of life in the West arose when we entered an abandoned town by the edge of New Mexico. There were a group of rabid Night Terrors along the mountain range. How they had managed to stay alive for so long was anybody's guess, maybe they had been drinking the water from the canyons and eating the fish.

We couldn't leave them running rampant in the desert. Lonnie and Kai headed to the nearest Elite Village to rent a truck. As an Elite, especially as a Berea, Lonnie had no limits to accessing resources. Kai concocted a scheme to acquire sedatives. He entered the Elite hospital and complained of insomnia. After noting where the doctor kept the supply, Kai snuck back in and stole a bunch. It was surprisingly easy for an Elite to commit a crime because no one expected them to.

We sedated the Night Terrors and put them in the back of the truck along with the bikes, and continued to the first rally in Arizona. Over one hundred people showed up to listen to my plan for a better future. I spoke for two hours, answering the Westerners' questions and becoming acquainted with their concerns. While all went accordingly with the rally, it didn't solve our issue with the Night Terrors. Most of the civilians who had come out had dispersed by then, and the five of us lingered by the truck discussing our options. We knew that the sedatives were wearing off as the sound of banging within the truck grew louder and louder.

"What are we going to do now?" Lee asked. "We can't just leave them in there. They are going to hurt themselves."

"I don't know. I have to think," I responded. There were three more rallies planned in the West. We couldn't keep the Night Terrors in the truck for the entire trip.

"We can find the nearest Village, and I can steal more sedatives," Kai suggested. It was the best plan we had.

Then out of the corner of my eye, I saw a woman walking toward us.

"Wonderful speech!" she exclaimed as she approached. She had long white hair braided into two pigtails that hung down past her waist. Her sombrero shielded her eyes from the sun, but the leathery skin around her eyes still wrinkled as she spoke. She invited us to her village, which was deep in the canyons of the desert. They had a private water source, their own solar panels for electricity, and best of all, an infirmary where they housed Sleepers. We handed over the Night Terrors to a group of civilians who secured them and led them away.

"They will be safe here," the woman assured us.

She invited us to stay for the night, and she organized an impromptu celebration for us. Her people were a friendly group, made mostly of Native Americans and Hispanics. She told us that the land they lived on was formerly a reservation. We sat around the campfire talking about everything from politics to family matters.

"We survived here for many years because we have been isolated from the outside world well before the gas attack," the woman spoke. "But being isolated is good only to an extent. We need resources ... medicine, food."

I told her, and her people that they wouldn't be forgotten when we took office and I meant it. That moment reminded me why I needed to venture out West, to hear these stories. She inspired me.

We left the reservation early the following morning. The truck was much more comfortable of a ride without the raging Night Terrors in the back. Pratt was driving, while Kai and I shared the front seat, and Lee was in a small back seat. Lonnie alternated from sitting in the middle to sitting beside Lee.

We had driven through Utah and Wyoming, each state offering a different type of beauty and serenity.

This trip had really opened my eyes to the vast differences each state had to hold. As a country, we were united by our brotherhood but as individual states we each had our own hurdles to overcome. I spoke with the civilians to familiarize myself with their struggles, and I got to see firsthand the destruction that this administration had done.

Our next rally was in Montana, then Iowa, and the last one in Illinois. After the rally in Montana, Pratt received one of his mysterious phone calls. He told us he had to head back to New York immediately, so he took one of the motorbikes and left. Kai shot me a sideways glance. Even Lonnie questioned Pratt's motives.

"Are you sure we can trust him?" Lonnie asked.

"He has never given us a reason not to. He's been with us from the start. Everybody is here because they believe in this movement," I assured her.

Lonnie accepted this explanation, but Kai shook his head and walked away. Deep down I also wondered what Pratt's motive for helping us was.

After the final rally, I was exhausted, but I couldn't stop thinking about the main concerns of each state. Montana had an ever-growing plastic pollution problem, Iowa's water quality crisis was killing people faster than the Night Terrors, and Illinois had a widespread measles outbreak due to a lack of access to vaccines. We were nearing the end of Indiana when I finally nodded off to sleep.

"We need gas," Lee noticed.

"Up ahead is the gas station," Lonnie said.

"We don't have clearance to stop there," Kai warned, gesturing to Lee and me. Gas stations were government-owned and manned by government officials. Not only was the government more than likely on the lookout for us, but Hoodlums weren't allowed to use any stores other than the Rations Center. We would be detained, and more than likely executed, if we were discovered.

"We will be fine," Lonnie said surely. "Let me drive. The rest of you hide in the back of the truck."

I wasn't as confident, however, but we didn't have a choice. It had been raining for the last twenty-four hours so the bikes wouldn't be charged. Our options were either to stop for gas or walk across the country back home to New York. The three of us covered ourselves with a blanket in the back of the truck and Lonnie drove into the station.

"ID Pass," the official said. He swiped her Pass.

"Okay, Miss Berea, how much?"

"Fill her up," Lonnie said, as she jumped out of the truck. She proceeded to walk into the store. While she was gone, the security officer poked around the truck.

"They're going to find us," Lee cried.

"Shut up," Kai whispered.

Lonnie strolled out of the store with fifteen meat sticks, two bags of chips, five sodas, and a gallon of water.

"What is it exactly that you are doing out here?" the official asked Lonnie suspiciously.

"That story is above your pay grade, pal," Lonnie replied, winking as she continued toward the truck. She climbed in and closed the door behind her. As she drove away, she rolled down her window and made a mock gun out of her fingers, shooting the two officials.

"It's all about confidence." I heard Lonnie say. I imagined the smirk that was on her face.

By the time we arrived back in Brooklyn, it was midnight. We parked the truck under the bridge and took the bikes into the city. Exhausted, we all trekked up to Kai's apartment to catch some much-needed sleep. As we entered, Lonnie turned on the lights.

"No, turn the lights off!" I cried, rushing to the window to draw the blinds tight.

"Why?" Lonnie asked.

"You can't leave the lights on at night. Either the Night Terrors or the Forces will see."

Lonnie was born and raised in Atlas. I knew she didn't understand the severity of that statement. "It could get us all *killed*," I added.

"For lights? Why?" she asked again.

"Because that's what happens. The Forces drive around at night looking for rebels. It would be highly suspicious to have a light on past midnight. And the Night Terrors are attracted to light. I don't know which would be worse."

"Oh, we don't have that problem in the Village. We stay up late and watch movies. Most dinner parties go well into the morning hours."

"Well, you're not at home. It's different here."

"I'm sorry."

I could tell she meant it. "It's not your fault," I said. It really wasn't her fault. There was no way for her to understand the life we lived from behind the wall.

I was both mentally and physically beat as I climbed into bed.

"No, it is," she replied, crawling under the sheets alongside me. "I act like I know the Divisions so well because I come out into it once a month to use the Rec Center. But you *live* it. It's different. It's not fair that people are just born to be in the Divisions or the Elite Villages."

"No, it isn't," I agreed. The conversation could have gone on longer, but my eyes began to close as the warmth from the blanket consumed me. "You know what else isn't fair?"

"What?" Lonnie asked.

"That you are hogging the bed," I grunted, gently nudging her over. "Let's try to sleep."

Lonnie smiled. She had become one of my best friends in such a short amount of time. I was so thankful to have my friends.

Chapter Fifteen

From that point on I never left my house without my security team. It was no surprise that Torrent didn't attempt an assassination during the debate because it was too public of an arena. But now that we were officially neck and neck in the polls, we knew she would attempt some malicious form of foul play.

When I rode out to Philadelphia for a rally, I had three cars, a motorbike brigade, and twelve horsemen armed and ready. I exited my car to cheers. The crowds had become so large that we had to hold rallies outdoors because few indoor spaces could hold the masses.

As I walked to the podium, I mingled with the people, shaking hands and kissing babies. As usual, I could almost feel the target on my head. I knew a Mule was going up to a room in a nearby building, setting up a sniper rifle, and focusing in on me. But I also knew my protector was on another roof nearby with a gun.

My protection was everywhere. I looked up and smiled directly at Conan, leader of the Hunters, who had zoomed in on me with his scope. Over one hundred men, including the Gangsters, Hunters, ex-military, and everyday folk, were part of my protection. Pratt stood lookout from a nearby building—my number one bodyguard.

The polls indicated that it was a tight race, but we couldn't rely on polls alone. We had to work those last few days to make sure that we gained enough votes to push us over the top. I knew that if we could convince people that the government was puppeteering the Sleepers, it would seal the win for us.

The puppets needed constant repetition to remember what to say, so a chip was on repeat in their ear at all times. Lonnie said that she could steal Gianna's chip from her father's office so that Kai could reprogram it. If Kai could change what Gianna was *hearing*, then it would change what she was *saying*. We could program her to expose the truth about Torrent on-air. Lonnie did what she promised, she stole the chip and brought it to Kai.

While Kai worked on the chip, Lonnie told him that the people in Atlas thought that his grandpa had killed him. She also said that his parents went missing soon after he did. Everyone assumed that the grandfather went crazy and killed them, too. That had been the story around the Elite Village, at least. Kai told me this one night before the news came on.

When the news started, we sat quietly in front of the vid, waiting to see Gianna. When she appeared, I think my heart stopped beating, and I am certain I stopped breathing until I heard the words escape her mouth.

"Torrent has brainwashed us. The Sleepers are the Puppets to her puppeteering. She cannot be trusted. There are more Puppets out there all around you ... the police, the politicians, and the celebrities. You must think for yourself. Do not allow the media and the Elites to misguide you. It's our time."

The broadcast quickly cut to another news program. It had worked!

Lonnie later told us that she had watched the news with her father. She had to hide her smile behind her teacup, as her father frantically called his engineers while the news played in the background.

I smiled, content with our work. The smoke and mirrors assembled by Torrent and her administration were taken away, at least briefly. Hopefully, it would be enough to persuade at least the few thousand more voters that we needed. Election day was only three days away.

Chapter Sixteen

I had to hide out for a couple of days. With the election so close in both time and numbers, there was a good chance Torrent would be coming for my head. We talked about heading to the Bedrock, but we thought it would be best to get out of the city. Pratt distracted the Mules by heading in the opposite direction, while Kai and I drove east to the Hamptons. No one would think to look for us there, and Pratt knew of a house that would be vacant.

"I just don't trust him," Kai sniffed.

"He's never given you any reason not to," I responded.

"Something about him just isn't right. I feel like he's hiding something. It's like he's a double agent or something."

"A double agent?" I looked at Kai from under my brows. I had to admit that he wasn't crazy for thinking it. This world was full of people with bad intentions, but there wasn't even a small part of me that thought Pratt was one of them. "He likes you," I lied. I wanted them to be friends. I trusted them both more than anyone else in the world.

"Oh yeah?" he laughed. "I think he likes *you*."

"Are you jealous?"

"Of what? His perfectly plucked eyebrows?" he scoffed.

"'Cause you sound jealous," I chuckled.

"El, I just don't want to see you get hurt."

I knew how he was feeling. All it would take was Pratt to tell one wrong person where we were, and we would both be dead. Not only that, but our movement would be squandered, and all that we had worked for would be gone. But I knew Pratt. I trusted him, even if I didn't have a reason to. Sometimes your gut knows whom you can trust. When we arrived at the house, we took a look around to make sure it was secure.

"This place is huge!" I said.

Kai looked around and mumbled, "Yeah, with plenty of hiding spots." He lifted his chin towards a stairwell that seemed to lead to a lower level. "We haven't checked down there yet."

We headed down the steps that led us to a large room with cedar walls. There in the center of the room was a luxurious swimming pool.

"Wow," he exclaimed.

"Yeah," I said, looking around. "Over there is the power." I pointed at the switchboard. There was a bunch of unlabeled buttons, and I had no idea what they did, so I shrugged and pushed them all. On went the underwater lights, the pool jets and filter, and even the music. Kai and I glanced at each other and laughed. I don't think either of us was expecting this.

"We are going in, right?" he asked.

"No! It's too cold," I objected, crossing my arms.

"It's heated!" Kai protested.

"Not yet it isn't. We just turned it on," I argued. "But be my guest, go in!"

"These Elites have pretty efficient heaters. I'm sure it's warm already." He gave me the most mischievous look I had ever seen on his face in my life.

"No," I repeated. I had meant to sound stern, but the face he was making was too comical for me to keep a straight face.

"I'll be mad!" I was trying harder to sound serious.

His smile didn't fade as he pushed me into the pool.

"No!" I screamed in vain as I hit the water. "Kai, you jerk!"

He immediately took his shirt off and jumped in, making a big splash right beside me. I pounced on him and tried to submerge his head underwater. He was a million times stronger than me, so I knew he was letting me win the wrestling match. As bubbles came up from the water, and his arms flailed, I couldn't help but laugh. I had forgotten who I was and what I was doing. For just a night I was simply a girl in her twenties again.

I fell asleep in the solarium under the stars, lying on Kai's chest. The sound of his heart and the waves put me to sleep as though both were competing to be the most peaceful. When I woke up, Kai wasn't next to me. I looked toward the balcony. He was outside under the stars looking up at the night sky. His blond hair was blowing in the breeze. His white shirt was open, and his white pants draped loosely on his body. I walked out onto the balcony. The sound of the ocean crashed as he turned to look at me. My heart skipped a beat.

"Hey," I said.

He smiled, as he pointed up to the sky. There was Orion's Belt and the Big Dipper vivid in the night sky. The Milky Way was clear, and a shooting star shot across the entire scene.

"Wow," I breathed, as I stared up at the sky.

Another shooting star went by. I sat down onto his lap. As we watched the meteor shower in silence, I knew there would never be a more beautiful moment in time. The stars shot across the sky one after another. The sound of the ocean waves crashing was near, along with the sound of Kai's breathing. I felt the warmth from his mouth on the back of my neck. I turned to him and tried to still my heart.

It would have been the perfect time for my first time. It would have been everything I had always pictured it to be, with the person I had always pictured it to be with. Our mouths moved closer, and our lips met. My heart pounded as his hands ran from my hair down to my neck, and then to my back. I gasped for air as I put my hands on his chest and felt his heart beating just as fast as mine. A thought of Pratt popped into my head. I pulled back quickly.

"What is it?" he asked, startled.

"Nothing."

But he was no fool. He knew something was wrong. I just hoped he didn't know exactly *what* it was. We both turned our eyes back up toward the sky. The silence was thick, and it would have been awkward if I were with anyone other than Kai.

"Are you hungry?" he asked.

"Starving, actually."

Food would do us both good. It had been a while since we had last eaten. I was glad he had thought of it because I probably would have forgotten to eat all together with everything going on. We headed up to the kitchen. Kai opened the cupboard to see what was on the menu. He rummaged through a few boxes.

"Pancakes or waffles?" he asked, as he turned to me with a box of instant pancake mix.

"Pancakes," I said smiling.

He amazed me as he showed off, flipping the pancakes like a pro. I laughed at the entertainment, thankful to have my mind off of the election. He came over to me with maple syrup in one hand and a plate of pancakes in the other.

"Someone order the lumberjack special?" he asked with a southern accent.

I laughed, taking the syrup from him. A drop of maple syrup dripped onto his finger, and I instinctively licked it off. I stopped and took a breath.

He was smiling down at me as I sat looking up at him when there was a knock at the door. We both heard it but stayed very still. Then Kai moved slowly to the counter and grabbed a large knife from the kitchen block. He was only about halfway to the door when we heard a voice.

"It's me." It was Pratt's voice.

"Pratt!" I exclaimed, walking past Kai to open the door.

Pratt smiled. Then he looked down and saw what I was wearing, just my underwear and a small top that exposed most of my mid-drift. I covered up a little. He looked past me and saw Kai wearing even less in only his boxers.

"Good morning …" he said slowly.

"What are you doing here?" I asked.

"I missed you."

"What are you doing here?" Kai repeated. "Do you know how stupid it was to come here? What if someone followed you?"

"No one followed me," Pratt said matter-of-factly.

"How do you know?" Kai asked with agitation in his voice.

"Because I know." Pratt seemed annoyed by Kai's distress.

"Yeah, you always just *know*. Tell me, Pratt, how is that?" Kai asked insistently. I could tell he was trying to provoke Pratt at that point and it appeared to be working.

"Is there something you want to accuse me of … or are you just upset because you wanted to have El all to yourself this weekend?" Pratt asked as he took a step forward into the room.

"No, I really want to know." Kai took a step toward Pratt.

"Guys, stop." I put a hand up in each of their directions. "Just stop!"

They both turned their eyes to me. Pratt's gaze took a little longer to deflect. "I can't do this without you two … the both of you. There is too much at stake right now, and you both know what's at risk if we lose." The plea in my voice was clear. I could tell they had both heard it.

"Okay," Pratt said, nodding. "I'll leave." He turned to walk away.

"No!" I exclaimed, louder than I had intended. Pratt turned back around to me.

"Stay," I begged. "Two days. In just two days it is going to be the most important day of our lives, no matter which way this election goes." I held his gaze for a moment. Then I turned to Kai.

"Can you both agree to get along?" Neither of them responded as I looked from Kai to Pratt. "For me?"

"Fine," Pratt replied, with a slight hostility in his voice.

Kai nodded and headed back to the breakfast bar to finish his pancakes.

I sighed. Keeping the peace between two men was difficult enough. I couldn't imagine how complicated keeping a nation at peace would be.

The day remained awkward, to say the least, but I made the best of it. We started putting together ideas for the new government. If we did win this election, we needed a team in place with a cabinet prepared. We drew out multiple boards and organization charts for each sector. I was considering keeping my security team employed even after the election. I didn't know how much I could trust the Secret Service after they had tried to kill me, and all. Even though they were bound by law to obey and protect the president, it was going to be a difficult thing to forget.

That night I slept in the master bedroom with Kai in the room next to me, and Pratt in the living room on the couch. I hadn't slept in such a big room by myself in, well, *ever*. It was haunting, really. The walls were so far away, and my thoughts bounced around in the empty space between them. I wanted to go stay with Pratt or Kai, but I didn't know which, so I crawled to the hallway in between the two of them and lay down. Kai found me there.

"What are you doing sleeping on the floor?" he asked.

"I wanted to come to your room or go to the couch, but I didn't know which one, so I just sat down here. In the middle."

Kai looked puzzled at first, and then he chuckled and shook his head. He knew I wasn't used to sleeping alone. "Come on. Let's all stay on the couch then."

And we did. I lay in the middle. It was the best sleep I had ever had.

Chapter Seventeen

We were awoken the following morning by the ividcam. Pratt was already out on the front porch when I looked out the window and saw Torrent's face projected onto the corner of the street.

"Good morning, citizens," the announcement began.

Kai and I wrestled the blankets off and went outside to join Pratt.

"On the eve of the election, I urge you to vote wisely. As your President, I have assured your safety and your survival through the Rations Centers and subsidized housing within the Divisions. As a nation, we have free health care for all citizens, and as a homeland, we have strengthened our borders to prevent another international attack," she said.

Kai and I shot each other a nervous glance.

"Now, some of you may be intrigued by Elisha Logan and her 'for the people' rhetoric, but let me assure you ..." she paused for effect, "it is all a show. El Logan is a *child,* and if you think for one moment, she is more than just that, you are mistaken. As President, El Logan would be more concerned with ... boys. But don't take it from me. Take it from her."

What is she up to?

I narrowed my eyes and saw Pratt do the same.

Torrent looked down and began to read, "'I can't deny my feelings for Kai; in a perfect world, I would be with him and only him forever. I think about it often, and it's like a fairytale ... he and I in the middle of nowhere, as husband and wife, maybe with some children. Pratt could never make me happy in that way.'"

Heart, don't stop beating. She was reading my diary on national vid. One of Torrent's minions must have found it. I immediately thought of my father and Lou. She continued to read:

"'Pratt is the opposite of Kai. Kai is honorable and good. Pratt has secrets, that much I can tell. But he is so damn sexy! It's the bad boy in him that intrigues me, but sometimes I wonder just how *bad* he is. Could Kai be right about him? Can Pratt be trusted? Everything inside me screams 'no.' If I had to choose right now between the two, it would be Kai.'" Torrent looked up at the camera.

"Aw, that's sweet. A little love triangle for Elisha. Let's hear her admission that she has no idea what she is doing."

Torrent turned back to the diary. "'I am a clueless, foolish girl who took on more than I can handle. This weight will surely be too much for me to carry on my own. I don't even know how to balance an asset account, never mind a national budget. I'm a fraud, and I have made fools of the people for believing in me.'"

Now I couldn't breathe. This was broadcasted on the One Network and played on every station and on every ividcam so that the entire country could hear.

"So, you see citizens, while Logan is having her prom date dilemma along with her identity crisis, I will be here for you, continuing to be the President you know and trust. Election Day is tomorrow. Vote wisely."

The ividcam shut down.

Kai retreated to the kitchen while Pratt remained on the front porch long after the announcement was over. The words Torrent read were indeed mine, but they were my personal thoughts, never meant for the ears of others. The way she read the words did them no justice. She cut and spliced them and turned them into a sort of summary of who I was, rather than what they were, just a free form expression of my feelings. I walked over to Pratt.

"Your family is okay," he said without looking at me.

"How do you know?" I asked.

He turned to me, and his solemn eyes widened as he shrugged. Then I remembered what I already knew, Pratt just always *knew*. I breathed a sigh of relief.

"I'm sorry you had to hear that," I said.

"Don't be. I'm sorry she read your diary on national vid." He was trying to seem unbothered by what he had just heard, but I knew his feelings were hurt.

"I write down my thoughts to help me process them. What comes out is not necessarily what I believe. The conclusion I come to after writing is often very different than just the string of words and ideas on paper."

"I know that," Pratt said. "But you were right."

"Right about what?"

"Me being a bad person."

"I didn't mean that—" I began, but he interrupted me.

"I didn't tell you everything when we were at your grandmother's house. I grew up in Somers with my brother. Our father was a military man, so the army was all I knew. I enlisted in the military when I was eighteen-years-old, and I was a good fighter, a loyal soldier. But when Torrent wanted me to kill innocent Americans, I couldn't. When things turned really bad my father formed a militia … my brother and I were part of it. At first, it was just to protect our homes, our families, and ourselves but eventually we knew Torrent was out of control.

"We started calling ourselves the Resistance. We knew we had to overturn the government. By that time, I was nineteen, and my brother was twenty-five. He was married, and he and his wife had a daughter,

Abigail. She was four. Other men, women, and children were part of the Resistance. They lived with us, too."

"In the Bedrock?" I asked.

"That was one of our hideouts, yes. But that isn't where we were staying at that time. We had been building up supplies in Somers, but things were getting bad up there. With no stores or Rations Centers within walking distance, and so few people with transportation, the crime in upstate New York was worse than the city. Groups of people formed tribe-like gangs and were killing people and pillaging houses left and right. A few groups had resorted to cannibalism.

"We were in the transition of moving our camp down to the Bedrock. My father, brother, and I had scouted out the area months earlier ... we knew it was safe and that we would have access to food and water, and most importantly, we would have a clear path to the Tower. The plan was to travel to Brooklyn, leave the children there with the people who were unable to fight, and head to Manhattan to a smaller outpost to prepare for the attack.

"In Manhattan, we had a safe spot directly under City Hall. It was an underground catacomb, part of a project from the late 1800s that was left unfinished. It was too small to stay there with our large group for too long, but we had to stop to assess our surroundings before making the crossing over the Brooklyn Bridge. We had fifty men and women in the militia, and there were twelve children including Abigail.

"I was out on a mission to scout for stationed soldiers when it happened. Torrent and her Mules found our camp. They killed everyone. When I came back to the catacombs, I found them all dead. My father and brother ...

"I vowed to kill Torrent myself. When I went to the Tower, the Mules didn't even put up a fight. They let me right in. And when I came face to face with Torrent, I didn't hesitate. I brought the barrel of my gun up to her head and then she said the words that made me who I am today."

He paused and swallowed hard. His clenched fists and tight jaw helped paint the scene for me.

"Torrent told me that it was *me* that the Mules were looking for ... that I was a deserter and the punishment was death. When they found our militia instead, they figured their deaths settled the score.

"She had Abigail. Abigail wasn't dead. They had taken her to live in Atlas with an Elite family. Torrent had hoped the memory of my brother and our family would fade for Abby, and she would go on to live a happy life.

"She told me that my family was criminals and that criminals have consequences for their actions. She promised, however, that Abigail wouldn't be harmed for my family's treason. If I worked for her and vowed my loyalty, she would spare Abby's life. To honor my brother, that's what I did. It was my fault that Torrent was looking for the militia. It's my fault they're all dead."

While I couldn't believe my ears, I sickened myself for not realizing it sooner. Now everything seemed so obvious.

"That's the phone call you got at my nana's cabin, isn't it? And that's how you knew about the air quality the day I met you." I began to put the pieces together. "*You.* You're the one who opened the exit door for me at Torrent Tower that day so I could escape." It all made sense now.

"I knew you were special from the moment I laid eyes on you," Pratt said. "You made me want to be a better person. That's why I protected you. That's why I made sure Torrent never got ahold of you."

I didn't respond. I was busy inside my head analyzing what I had just learned. Kai was right about Pratt all along, he *was* a double agent. But he was also Pratt.

"I don't expect you to forgive me. I don't expect anything from you. Kai is a good man, and you two are lucky to have each other," he said, and then he turned and walked down the steps. He didn't look back. I watched him climb into his truck and drive away.

I stood in the kitchen for a long while, replaying the details of our time together in light of this new information. It changed everything in the smallest, but most intrinsic way. Pratt had protected me in more ways than I knew. He was right that I wouldn't have trusted him had I known he was a Mule. But I *had* trusted him, so the question was now, could I forgive him, a man who worked for Torrent, that evil tyrant, and then lied to me about it? Even if it was to save his niece, it seemed to be unforgivable.

My deep thoughts were interrupted by a phone call. It was Theo. He said he had received a call yesterday telling him to rush our family out of the apartment. An assailant team was headed his way. Theo said that the voice on the other end of the line refused to say who they were. They only said that he had minutes before the Forces arrived, so Theo and Sanzhar headed to the rooftops to confirm what they had heard. Sure enough, a convoy of Forces was headed toward the apartment. They went to warn Dad, but my father was stubborn and wanted to stay and fight.

"You and what army?" Theo asked. Dad was a good fighter. He fought in more than one battle, but with his punctured lung and the number of soldiers heading their way, even with the help of the BK12, they were no match. Theo and Sanzhar took my family to the BK12 hideout, where Nan told stories to the Gangsters. By the time the Forces arrived at the apartment, my family was gone. *That must have been when they found my diary.*

But my family was safe thanks to the familiar voice on the other end of the line, and that was what mattered the most.

Chapter Eighteen

The people had spoken.

The election of 2046 was a landslide victory for the Laissez-Faire. There was no concession speech, not even a word from Torrent or her staff. All was eerily quiet from Torrent Tower. A brigade of cars, trucks, bikes, and horses had made its way out to the house on the ocean where Kai and I were staying. There was a knock on our door. I opened it wide to reveal Sheriff Chaplin, the Hunters, BK12, and my family and friends, all those who helped me get where we were today.

"You ready to go to the Tower, Madam President?" Sheriff Chaplin asked.

I smiled at him. I looked at the group behind him, my Hunters and Gangsters were on one side, and the U.S. Secret Service was on the other.

"They are an obedient group, as the aptitude test ascertained," Sheriff Chaplin said. "They vow loyalty to the elected President ... that went for Torrent, and now that goes for you. Now you can accept that, or you can fire them, that is up to you."

I wasn't sure if I was in the mood to fire anyone at that very moment, but I had time to consider my options. I moved slightly to my right to look around Sheriff Chaplin. I saw Pratt leaning up against his truck.

"Pratt!" I yelled. I ran over to him and wrapped my arms around his waist. I was so relieved to see him.

"I guess I'm forgiven," Pratt smiled.

"Forgiven? You made this possible. Without you," I looked up at everyone standing around us and spoke louder. "Without *all* of you, this wouldn't be possible."

I looked around at the group of people that surrounded me, the ones who were there from the beginning, and the ones who stood with us now. It was a diverse crowd, but they all had one thing in common, they were clapping. They weren't applauding me; their clapping was a sign of hope. I watched the hands of my friends, the Secret Service, and my family, hands that had once fought one another now clapped in unison. We could start a new beginning in harmony.

"Come on. Let's all go to the Tower," I declared, walking over to the passenger side of Pratt's truck.

"Why don't you jump in with the Sheriff," Pratt suggested.

"You're coming with me, aren't you?" I asked.

"There is somewhere I need to be. But I will meet up with you later."

I nodded and felt Sheriff Chaplin's hand on my shoulder. As I turned, I was greeted with his smile as he reached to shake my hand. The BK12 jumped on their scooters and skateboards, while the Hunters mounted their motorbikes and horses. Kai, Lonnie, Lee, and I walked over to the cop car.

"You guys don't mind if I sit in front, right? I got sick the last time I rode in the back of one of these," Lee groaned. The rest of us squeezed into the back of the car.

"Nice way to start your presidency," Lonnie joked, winking at me. "Put the sirens on, Sheriff Chaplin!"

In New York City, Torrent and her assistant were riding in the back of her armored limo. Torrent was thinking out loud while Bruna took notes.

"We have to do *something*. Gather up a team to have her killed, maybe. How can we make it look like an accident? We must get the people back on our side. We will have to make it look like the rival gangsters killed her, perhaps in a power struggle."

The limo stopped short. They were supposed to be heading to the Elite Village of Spire, but it appeared that they were in the inner city of Division 1, right along the edge of New York City bordering the Hudson River.

"Where the hell are we?" Torrent asked.

The window between the rear seats and driver section rolled down.

"Hello ladies, gentlemen," said Pratt.

Bruna narrowed her eyes at the remark.

"Elk, where are we?" Torrent asked.

"I have something to tell you," Pratt said, or as Torrent called him, Elk. He told her exactly what she had once said to El.

"You're not going to be needed anymore. Your little show … it's over. You're going to find a spot in some valley somewhere, and you are going to live and die there … alone or with your … Bruna. It doesn't matter. Because *you* don't matter. But let's make one thing very clear. You will never again see the inside of the White Tower. Ever." Pratt paused for a moment. "Now, get out," he ordered, and he turned around.

Torrent looked out of the window and realized they were in the middle of the ghetto.

"Don't be ridiculous, Elk. What about Abigail?" she asked pompously.

"Abby is safe somewhere where you can't touch her." He had made arrangements with Lonnie to have her picked up from the Charter School and taken to the White Tower.

Torrent looked outside once again. She fiddled with her briefcase. "I can transfer you money. Just say the number. I have unlimited funds. How much do you want?" She took out her phone and went to tap her bank scanner.

"I wouldn't be so sure about that."

The number, which was once so long that it took up multiple lines on the balance sheet was now a big round zero. "What is this?" she asked as she refreshed the bank scanner. When the number remained at zero with each reset, she began pressing the screen on the phone frantically. "No!"

"Oh, yes," Pratt chirped. "We made arrangements to fund research and development programs with the money from the Elites' bank accounts, yours included. We will be starting over, and you'll be starting at zero.

"You should be thankful, because if it were up to me ..." Pratt paused and thought about his next words carefully. "I've dreamed of making you suffer, a slow, agonizing dehumanizing death as you have done to so many millions of people. But El didn't want it that way. So, I'll leave it up to you. We will be watching you. We are everywhere. And if anything happens ... if you even lift your littlest finger to try and pull anything ... I won't hesitate to make my dream true." He stared into Torrent's eyes for a solid ten seconds, daring her to respond. He turned around in his seat. "Now get out. I have somewhere to be. Hurry up." He drummed his fingers on the steering wheel and watched her in the rearview mirror.

Torrent placed her hand on the door handle and opened her mouth to object, but when she caught Pratt's fiery eyes in the mirror, she closed her mouth quickly. She opened the door and stepped out of the armored limo and into the mercy of the masses.

Torrent looked toward Bruna for help, but Bruna quickly darted into the crowd, which had formed when they recognized her car, and slipped away. Bruna's face was far less recognizable than Torrent's. Torrent, on the other hand, had no option to slip away. The crowd knew her face well from every time its hologram was beamed into the sky.

She took a look at the wrathful crowd around her. The people she had once ruled over and looked down upon now looked down upon her. She had no choice other than to begin a slow walk through the crowd. They barely made a passage for her.

A woman holding her infant child spit on Torrent and yelled, "Get to your knees!" Her irate scream promoted others to do the same.

The screams weren't as bad as the whispers, however, which were loud enough for Torrent to hear. They were talking about killing her. She cowered her head and began to snivel as she dropped to all fours and crawled through the swarm of people.

Pratt looked on, but only for a moment. He remembered where he really wanted to be.

With his friends.

With us.

Chapter Nineteen

The new world.

I can't say that I won because I didn't.
We did.

I wouldn't have been able to accomplish any triumphs over the past year without the help of my family, Pratt, Kai, Lonnie, Lee, Gianna, Sheriff Chaplin, and my security team. Each of these people has a role in the new administration. Sheriff Chaplin is Captain of the Police Commission.

We reinstated the original Constitution of the United States. Well, except for Article Two Section One about having to be age thirty-five or older to be president, of course.

Lonnie's knowledge of six languages turned out to be not so useless, after all. After the election, I appointed her Lead Ambassador of International Relations.

It is safe to say that the rest of the world had been furious at the United States for a long time, pinning an apocalypse on Russia didn't sit well with any country in the United Nations, or otherwise. There was no way we could make right the level of wrong we had reached, but we did distribute the cure for cancer as a symbol of renewed world leadership and trust.

The cure was found using Dr. Maxwell's old laboratory notebook. He had begun working on a cure for cancer that took a damaged cell and turned back the mutation, like turning back a clock. The medicine worked through inhalation, just like the gas. In theory, a person would breathe in the chemical compound and the agents would enter the bloodstream and search for damaged DNA. The mutated DNA would be detected and cloaked by an agent that is both destructive and regenerative. Meanwhile, a cloning agent would replicate intact DNA, and clone it onto the cloaked DNA, permanently repairing all signs of disease. Tissue must be alive for the components to work, and the cure won't prevent natural aging.

Kai and Lee worked in the lab to use the same formula to create a cure for the Sleepers. With one formula, thanks to Kai's grandfather, as well as Kai and Lee, we were able to cure both cancer and Sleepers. The antidote was administered via military aircraft over every nation in the world. Dr. Maxwell was right—science could change the world.

Kai could change the world.

Pratt, other than being my fiancé, oversees the military. From the first time I saw him, he intrigued me and every day after that has been an adventure with him. He isn't polished, pretty, or sophisticated but he is funny, dependable, charming, and although I tried to fight it, he stole my heart somewhere along the way. He, along with the reinstated army generals who were imprisoned under Torrent's rule, have been working on rebuilding the American Navy, Air Force, Marines, and Army.

Gianna is my Press Secretary. Although many of her colleagues questioned my decision to appoint a reformed Sleeper as Press Secretary, I can assure you our antidote left no trace of any puppeteering.

Theo and the BK12 weren't forgotten. They each took jobs, some in construction, agriculture, and technology, but many chose to remain part of my Secret Service. Theo chose to take a position in the school as an economics teacher. He always did have an interest in the production and transfer of wealth.

Most of the Hunters wanted to continue to hunt. Some stayed on my security team, and others opened butcher shops and grocery stores across the country. Conan was promoted to head of my security detail.

Lou and Abigail attend a great school. They are a few grades apart, but they've become the best of friends. We have teachers and students at a one to ten ratio, and the smaller classrooms allow the teachers to focus on each student as an individual. Abigail is taking sign language courses, and I hear Lou is reading *To Kill a Mockingbird*.

One of the first orders of business was to tear down the walls of the Elite Villages around the nation. All three-hundred and fifty Village wall enclosures were demolished, and the cities were restored.

Logan and Co., my father's company, led the nation in construction and infrastructure. The company is now in every state, along with numerous other construction companies, of course, since the free market and capitalism were reinstated immediately. With this, small businesses started to flourish. Soon we were seeing coffee shops and delis popping up in the larger cities and then smaller cities alike.

My family stayed right there at 25 Valley Street in Brownsville, with a little modification to the apartment building, of course. Dad knocked down a few walls in the apartment. The entire second floor, which included six bedrooms, three bathrooms, a grand dining room, two large living rooms, and an office, was now home to Dad, Nan, Theo, and Lou with enough room for Pratt, Abigail, and I to stay in the guest rooms when we visited. Nan has a large window in her room with her very own balcony where she prefers to drink her morning coffee nowadays.

Kai and Summer, Conan's daughter, live together as a couple in the White Tower with Pratt and I. When I invited the leaders of New Hudson to the Tower, Kai fell in love with her at first sight. Her long red hair and bright green eyes were quite striking. She was also one heck of a leader. Her village in the New Hudson proved to be the most successful of all the settlements, attracting colonizers from around the nation. New York was flourishing once again, and the entire nation was beginning to rebuild. We intend to have an election in four years.

We still have work to do. We are far from being the country we want to be, but we are getting closer to it every day. Many of us have done things in our life that we aren't proud of. In a world where we were forced to kneel for so long, we forgot how to stand. Still, we fought back against the powers that held us down, and we won. Now we stand, and we won't ever kneel helplessly again.

We are one nation built by and for each other. We will have each other's backs, and we will look out for one another. Should any form of tyranny try to rain down on this country, we will unite and fight again, until all dictators, and all enemies of democracy and freedom will understand that the American Dream isn't a dream at all.

It's our families. It's our friends. It's our communities. It's our lives. It's our time.

It's our time!

Epilogue

In an underground facility, deep within the sands of the Chihuahua Desert in New Mexico, Torrent and a small camp of Mules and resentful Elites dwelled. A map lay flat upon a metal table with Torrent and her new top aid, Kido, standing over it.

"There is one thing that those Hoodlums didn't account for," Torrent seethed from behind the table.

Kido stood anxiously across from a grinning Torrent.

The map was no ordinary map, rather one drawn specifically to prevent global eradication. When Torrent was president, and she took over the universal satellite grid, she also took control of every active nuclear weapon that could be detonated via satellite. There were fifty weapons in total, enough to wipe mankind off the face of the earth completely. Even her own team believed that the power was too much for any one person to have at their fingertips.

Torrent's lead scientists recoded each satellite with a specific set of numbers and hid the codes in secret bunkers in different locations around the nation. And if one day Torrent were to launch a global nuclear attack, each individual code would have to be retrieved first. The map showed the locations of each of the fifty hidden vaults around the country that contained the codes for nuclear annihilation.

"Get over here, dimwit," Torrent yelled to one of her soldiers.

As the top-heavy soldier waddled steadily over, Torrent pointed to the map. "Find me these codes and bring them to me."

The soldier took the map and scampered away.

"If we detonate the bombs, we won't have any citizens to rule over," Kido fretted as he twiddled his thumbs. Kido wasn't the first person to take Bruna's place as Torrent's top aide. Her last assistant was fired, and by fired, I mean killed, due to a perceived lack of enthusiasm for the position. There was one feature Torrent valued more than power—subservience. The two went hand in hand for her. Even in this sinkhole, she demanded respect, focus, and blind loyalty.

"Fool! I know that," Torrent bellowed. "We aren't going to detonate all of the bombs. We need only detonate those pointed at the largest cities, Brooklyn, Los Angeles, Detroit, Washington D.C, and Houston. That will get their attention. Those who don't die will fear me."

Kido nodded along with her. He was a man of average height with long blonde hair that was pulled back into a low ponytail. His thick dark glasses sat low on his nose, and he was always pushing them up with a long bony finger.

"I tried to rule by love, but would they have it? No. They would rather that infantile imbecile lead them!" She clenched her fist, and she heaved the words from her throat. "Now they will see just what it means to suffer."

The words lingered in the air without follow up. The silence grew longer, and when Kido began to pick the remnants of some past meal out of his teeth with both his tongue and fingers, Torrent shot him a glance that implied he better respond if he wanted to live. He dropped his hand and retreated his tongue swiftly.

"Oh, yes. They'll fear you all right. They'll be so afraid they won't be able to sleep at night." Kido snickered.

Torrent, seemingly pleased with Kido's response, raised her chin and began to walk away. She hadn't made it five feet before Kido spun around and called out to her, lost without his master.

"What should we do in the meantime, Madam?" Kido pleaded.

Torrent paused, and then spun around.

"Recruit me more Mules," she ordered. "The bunkers will be guarded, so we must act fast. Our military assets are still in place. They haven't been replaced by that little bitch's team yet."

"Soon she will destroy the codes or worse, she will give the satellites back to their original owners," Kido added.

"Correct, Kido. You have a brain in there after all," Torrent said. "Now ... more Mules!"

Diane Krauss

Diane Krauss was born and raised by her nurturing mother and hardworking father, alongside her two older sisters in the Hudson Valley of New York. Books were always a treasure for Diane so she collected and stashed as many as she could in her closet as a child and would spend hours reading to her sisters, or stuffed animals— whoever would listen.

She was a preschool teacher and activist before getting married in 2017 to her sweetheart and love of her life, Mark. She began writing her first young adult novel while on their honeymoon backpacking through Europe after discussing politics with the locals in small villages throughout each country.

Diane still lives in New York's Hudson Valley where she continues to write children stories. She lives with her husband, their two huskies and their son, Kai, who she considers to be the greatest treasure of all.

Reader's Guide

1. After reading It's our Time, do you agree with the author's choice she made for El between Kai and Pratt? Why?
2. If you were El, would you have chosen Kai or Pratt? Why?
3. How does El's father change throughout the novel?
4. Does El's rise to power change her moral outlook? If so, how does she change?
5. What happens to the Sleepers?
6. What happens to the Night Terrors?
7. Given today's political climate, how does El's behavior of appointing her friends and family to important positions mirror today's administration? Does it make her any different from Torrent?
8. What governs Kai's actions?
9. If Pratt, as Elk, has so much power and influence, why didn't he just take his niece back himself?
10. What do you think swayed the public to vote for El instead of Torrent?
11. Do you think that the events that happened in this novel could happen in America today?
12. What would move you to rebel against your government?
13. How would you deal with the Elites if you became President in the novel?
14. Which character is your least favorite? Your most favorite? Why?
15. Why not just kill off Torrent? Why does El allow her to live?

A Note from the Publisher

Dear Reader,

Thank you for reading Diane Krauss' novel, *It's Our Time*.

We feel the best way to show appreciation for an author is by leaving a review. You may do so on any of the following sites:

www.ZimbellHousePublishing.com
Goodreads.com
or your favorite retailer

Join our mailing list to receive updates on new releases, discounts, bonus content, and other great books from Diane Krauss and

Or visit us online to sign up at:
http://www.ZimbellHousePublishing.com

CPSIA information can be obtained
at www.ICGtesting.com
Printed in the USA
LVHW110727231219
641443LV00007B/198/P